BERG

BERG

Ann Quin

SHEFFIELD – LONDON – NEW YORK

This edition published in 2019 by And Other Stories
Sheffield – London – New York
www.andotherstories.org

First published in Great Britain in 1964 by Calder and Boyars Ltd

9 8 7 6 5

This book is a work of fiction. Any resemblance to actual persons, living or dead, events or places is entirely coincidental.

ISBN: 978-1-911508-54-0
eBook ISBN: 978-1911508-55-7

Proofreader: Sarah Terry; Typesetter: Tetragon, London; Typefaces: Linotype Swift Neue and Verlag; Cover Design: Edward Bettison. Printed and bound by the CPI Group (UK) Ltd, Croydon, CRO 4YY.

A catalogue record for this book is available from the British Library.

Supported using public funding by

ARTS COUNCIL ENGLAND

MIX
Paper from
responsible sources
FSC® C171272

For Mother

A man called Berg, who changed his name to Greb, came to a seaside town intending to kill his father . . .

Window blurred by out of season spray. Above the sea, over-looking the town, a body rolls upon a creaking bed: fish without fins, flat-headed, white-scaled, bound by a corridor room – dimensions rarely touched by the sun – Alistair Berg, hair-restorer, curled webbed toes, strung between heart and clock, nibbles in the half light, and laughter from the dance hall opposite. Shall I go there again, select another one? A dozen would hardly satisfy; consolation in masturbation, pornographic pictures hanging from branches of the brain. WANTED one downy, lighthearted singing bird to lay, and forget the rest. A week spent in an alien town, yet no further progress – the old man not even approached, and after all these years, the promises, plans, the imaginative pursuit as static as a dream of yesterday. The clean blade of a knife slicing up the partition that divides me from them. Oh yes I have seen you with her – she who shares your life now, fondles you, laughs or cries because of you. Meeting on the stairs, at first the hostile looks, third day: acknowledgment. A new lodger, let's show him the best side. Good morning, nice day. Good afternoon, cold today. His arm linked with hers. As they passed Berg nodded, vaguely smiled, cultivating that mysterious air of one pretending he wishes to remain detached, anonymous. Afterwards their laughter bounced back, broke up the walls, split his door; still later the partition vibrated, while he paced the narrow strip of carpet between wardrobe and bed, occasionally glimpsing the reflection of a thin arch that had chosen to represent his mouth. Rummaging under the mattress Berg pulled out the beer-stained piece of newspaper, peered at the small photograph.

Oh it's him Aly, no mistaking your poor father. How my heart turned, fancy after all this time, and not a word, and there he is, as though risen from the dead. That Woman next to him Aly, who do you suppose she is?

He had noticed the arm clinging round the fragile shoulders; his father's mistress, or just a friend? hardly when – well when the photo showed their relationship to be of quite an affectionate nature. Now he knew. It hadn't taken long to inveigle his way into the same house, take a room right next to theirs. Yes he had been lucky, everything had fallen into place. No hardship surely now in accepting that events in consequence, in their persistent role of chance and order, should slow down?

Meanwhile he'd find out how they lived, the time they actually spent together. One more clue today: a letter on the hall table, addressed to Mrs. Judith Goldstein, room 19; where then Mr. Goldstein – a hundred feet deep, or perhaps only twenty feet away, yet someone else betrayed, scheming, scratching behind another wall? Berg pushed back the newspaper cutting under the mattress, and sat on the edge of the bed, head reclined from the eclipse that settled over the room, rumpled bed, the chest of drawers, that refused to close; the half open wardrobe doors, the chipped enamel pot with its faded blue flowers; the wallpaper making everything else collide; this morning's dirty dishes, half a brown loaf – a monk's cowl – perched on the pale yellow plastic table cloth; pin-striped trousers over the rose-chintz chair; pants, string vests; the case full of bottles, wigs, pamphlets: BUY BERG'S BEST HAIR TONIC DEFEAT DELILAH'S DAMAGE: IN TWO MONTHS YOU WILL BE A NEW MAN. Beside the bed, piled neatly, letters from Edith Berg, devoted unconditionally to her only son:

> Oh Aly I don't like you going off to see him like this. I'm sure it's not the proper thing to do, I mean he won't ever recognise you, let alone acknowledge you after all these years.

Through a gap in the curtain, made by one stained finger, and if parted wide enough for a spider to slide through, Berg could watch the illuminated palace across the road lighting up the solid Victorian blocks, surrounded by parked vehicles. On the right a triangular patch of churchyard; perhaps that's what accounted for the burnt smell that invaded his room every night, if some paper was stuffed in the cracks, and he remembered to close the window, then the smell might be kept out. He pulled the window right down, and remained gloating over the couples that entered the dance hall. Once he had ventured across, and brought back a giggling piece of fluff, that flapped and flustered, until he was incapable, apologetic, a dry fig held by sticky hands. Well I must say you're a fine one, bringing me all the way up here, what do you want then, here are you blubbering, oh go back to Mum. Lor' wait until I tell them all what I got tonight, laugh, they'll die. Longing to be castrated; shaving pubic hairs. Like playing with a doll, rising out of the bath, a pink jujube, a lighthouse, outside the rocks rose in body, later forming into maggots that invaded the long nights, crawled out of sealed walls, and tumbled between the creases in the sheets. Beyond this a faint recollection of a grizzled face peering over, being lowered, on string, to kiss – but no surely to smother you? Edith calling, stifled giggles with Doreen; wanting desperately to go some-where, how it had come, a shower of golden rain over her new scarlet dress. Later Uncle Billy, home on leave, drunk, drenched with sweat and tobacco smells, drawing you over his knees; kissing taboo, you just confirmed, it's dirty, not the thing to do, leads to other things. Like photos of nudes, Nicky and Bert kept pasted in their scripture books, relieving the laceration of Miss Hill's vagina; spinsterhood personified, with her sadistic fascination for boys' backsides. Alistair Berg come here, bend over please.

Darkness, radio on. Inside something stirred – a child murmuring in its sleep. A moth bumped against the wall, the door, the light. Berg's fingers strayed, lingered on the switch. The moth sizzled against the bulb, now wingless fell. The stairs creaked, could it be the old man, by himself? Berg switched the light off, and opened the door a little. Striking a match he waited, unaware that the flame licked his hand. A movement nearby, followed by a woman's voice. Soon Judith appeared, groping her way along by the landing walls. Berg heard the jingle of keys, the sound of their door being opened, closed.

She was, without doubt, a good deal younger than his father, attractive, he supposed, in the artificial style, and who would wish to go beyond the surface in a woman anyway? But what did she see in the old man, certainly not the lure of money, to all intents and purposes he seemed to be living on and off her. A form of mutual perversion? But their sex life hardly concerned him, not at the moment anyway; let the interpretation of their relationship remain in the abstract.

He must present himself one evening, suggest a drink, which would certainly be taken up by his father; every night the old man stumbled up the stairs, followed by raised voices for half an hour or more, then the creaking of their bed the other side for hours, literally hours, while he buried himself under the blankets.

He yawned, stretched; the music distracted, he went to the window. A microscopic eye upon a never-changing scene, except perhaps the weather. Youths nonchalantly leaned from the windows, behind them twisting shapes of couples could be seen, and as from an umbilical cord Berg strung himself through their weaving arms and legs. An eye, then two, stared across. He pulled the curtains, and leaned against the wall, choking over a cigarette. Gradually he calmed down, and pushed his face against the window. Another eye gazed as through a telescope, held his own, then fell. He faced the room. Why get into such a state, just because someone had seen him, surely there was nothing to fear, nothing to be ashamed of? He drew back the curtains, the lights swirled in and round every available object, frantically searching for something, heard of perhaps, but never allowed to see. Berg remained in one beam of light, trying hard not to expose the internal rustle, or lay bare the final draft: abide by the rules and regulations of your chosen part; surrendered, sealed. Full signature here please ALISTAIR CHARLES HUMPHREY BERG, born third of the third, nineteen hundred and thirty-one. Father's profession: gentleman of unknown origins, scoundrel of the first order. Mother: lady of unequalled measure, mother of genius . . .

Now you're out of the Army Aly you'll have to find a job.

At seventeen discovered to be sterile, followed by secret injections: incurable. But think of the others, those who inevitably fulfil their obligations, he was one of the lucky ones, be thankful for small mercies, at least he wasn't impotent.

> Well my boy what are you thinking of taking up eh, following in your father's footsteps I suppose, or is it the Civil Service – they look after you well there you know?

No denying that, never forgotten once filed away, numbered, documented. Respectability was what Edith had regard for, expected of him to be a good, solid-working citizen.

> You see I've never had the better things in life Aly. Of course I don't expect you to understand, but what I haven't had I want you to have.

The martyred airs, the coughing, sometimes all night long, over the weekends; a special shave, blunt blades, her pleasure in putting on the dabs of cotton wool.

> When will you be down again Aly? Now you know that's not true, I'm just wondering that's all, as I like to know, but then you have your own life to lead, and I'll not stand in your way.

Confronted by her flushed face from the neck up, her hands fluttering; the faded brilliance of a saved-up birthday brooch on her nylon-fur coat lapel, the rusty pin at the edge that always caught something in your throat; the tear-glazed eyes, intake of breath not allowed to escape until the train's steam merged with the clouds going West. Screwing his eyes up,

Berg lay back; the waves of jazz, or a slow waltz crowded in upon the necropolis of cells, like hard-polished beads, one pull, how far would they roll? You see if I tried explaining – no it isn't any use, why the continual persistence to lubricate the conscience?

Time meaningless for you exploring the mysterious regions of mountains, lakes, jungles within a blanket territory. I pull my eye through a keyhole, on a string the days are declared; thoughts are switchbacks uncontrolled.

Threading experience through imaginative material, acting out fictitious parts, or choosing a stale-mate for compromise. Under this fabrication a secret army gathers defeating those who stalk the scaffolding of comparisons. Yet they still haunt with their pale perplexities, and resentful airs. Then you had nothing to give, apart from a spinning top once seen, or a blue windmill worshipped. Idea and image juxtapositioned, spinning between myth and rationality, the odd years spent at a right angle; if I over-reach, can I be sure of reclaiming a formula outside habitual movement? How easy it would be to finally slide over, allowing the rest to absolve itself. But remember society owes you nothing, therefore, doing yourself in isn't the answer, no reward for the resentment, and how would I know if it had proved freedom? Remember the swings, the shoots, and roundabout horses; dizzy and dazzled, sticky fingers on a stray cat, a dead thrush, a rabbit stunned; cornflowers sprayed against stained glass; poppies in cornfields, the first, second, or was it the third kiss given, not on the lips, in the hay; rats scuttling, and the kisses later chalk-marked on park benches: I've got the most. Days of sun and smells of home-made cakes, toffee, fallen apples; Edith's face haloed in the blitzed outhouse window. You digging, climbing, dressing up, poking tongues, touching one another there, what would they say if they knew? Hills meeting sky, and those who charmed paths with snails, or put Catherine wheels in hedges; rockets misfired from other planets; the whole galaxy: a giant's chair, oneself a splinter in the leg. Daisy-chained to the girl next door, and envious of those who held between their legs a bigger daffodilly than your own.

Aware that the clock had stopped Berg switched the light on. Without knowing the time he felt out of orbit. He strained against the partition. Were they in bed yet, had someone coughed? He went to the window, the dance hall closed down, which indicated it was well past eleven. He leaned out, but failed seeing the pub clock. Very well he'd wait until a clock struck. He looked through the accounts, but these proved too depressing. He flicked through a magazine, stared for a time at the girl soaping herself in a turquoise-coloured bath. Yes he might have done better in the soap line, large lemon-shaped ones, held out to neglected house-wives, giving them, himself pleasure for a stipulated time. Hair-growth after all only interested men. Apply twice nightly, feel its satin-smooth goodness. Then why haven't I a lion's mane, and roaring round the town? The partition, hadn't it moved? He pressed against it. Were they both just the other side, the old man, mole-like, crawling over her mounds of flesh? Use the excuse of enquiring the time, the clock as evidence.

Knocking on their door, a panther's paw that rubbed until it became a pounding no one responded to. He tried the handle. They were there all right, fancy pretending like that, it wasn't as if he had disturbed them from sleeping. He coughed, and gasped, while walking rapidly up and down the landing. Should he go back into his room, shout from there, scream in fact, as though in the middle of a nightmare? He remained at the top of the stairs, cut off from the rest of the house, the neighbourhood. Had they gone out, or were they dead – copulating too fast, too much? He moved down one stair head bowed considering the best way into the next event. The other doors had, during his stay, remained part of the walls, a slight murmur or hum of a radio escaped occasionally through a crack. But if he knocked, enquired the time, wouldn't the crack immediately be sealed, not even space for an eye, let alone his finger? He hovered on the front door step, two hundred yards from the Palais de Dance. Coloured tickets, spent out balloons, contraceptives divided pavement from road. Berg leaned slightly forward in order to see the pub clock. On his back he stared at the buildings that were giants advancing. Snatch the stars, pull out the moon for my navel, a button hole for my own personal identification.

A shadow pushed itself across his face. He spread out his arms. I implore to be left where I am, as I have been given, I am satisfied, attuned to my world. He shut his eyes, and foetus-curled from the pavement. His lips dry leaves slowly parted. Have I ever been inside?

Edith's tears, not coping, timid amongst robust mums. You discovered: dormitory pleasures, what is considered a pretty boy at the age of nine, to be taken advantage of.

> Oh Aly I would rather you had died than bring me this dreadful shame, this terrible sorrow. I don't understand the evil lust in you, you've taken all the joy out of my life.

Round scarred knees, hair that curled; he's a cissy, just a common cissy; hasn't got a dad, his mum pawns herself to pay the fees; silly cissy Berg, he's so cold he can't even crap. Was it a game then, to be given something, have it taken away sooner or later? He placed his fist in the palm of his hand, contemplating it, as though a pimento that might suddenly open, reveal other more delicious things. Could the exterior world denounce him, when he was so willing to resign – but are you that willing? Contradictions seemed the very symbiosis of an age that refused accepting a one-way ticket to no-man's land. I've torn mine up a long way back, in gardens, smooth terraced lawns, butterflies and rare specimens of flowers, lying there, spying through channels of light that flickered on the boy who was left the other side of the hedge. A sticky sickly child, who longed to be accepted with the others, by those who were healthy, tough, swaggered in well-cut suits, brilliantined hair. Your stained, rat-bitten cuffs, and collar, patched behind, the mud squelching through your shoes. But once on your own when you lorded it with beast and flower, striding the hills, welcomed by a natural order, a slow sensuality that circled the sun, rode the wind through the grass-forests, then nothing mattered, because everything comprehended your significance. He swayed in the middle of the road, looking into his father's eyes; eyes that rolled inwards, joined by a thread through the bridge of his nose, run off from the mole on his right cheek with its one dark hair. Berg stepped back, away from the smell of alcohol and stale tobacco. The old man tottered a little towards him, trying to roll a cigarette. Hey wait a minute, aren't you the chap who's taken the room next door, Number 18? Yes thought it was, had a bit too much yourself I see, well why not I say, gives a chap a break doesn't it? Tongue along paper, a lizard hesitating, then flick, flick of its tail, gone. That I come from this? No, no should have rested with the image of a mellow self-respecting father, who had died in thought alone. The plan had worked too well, almost accidentally, surely to be mistrusted: the beast without the reins? But I must go on, as before, as planned. Disclosure of identity now would be fatal. Berg took hold of the old man's arm, but found himself pushed firmly away. All right, all right I can manage thanks. He watched his father stumble towards the house.

Such an opportunity squandered. Even now he could pick a fight, antagonise the old chap, in a matter of seconds he would be stretched out. And the remains? Well he would remain, wasn't that enough? But like a love affair, it seemed too easy, therefore, the preliminaries must be prolonged; flirt a little with the opportunities. There he was lurching in the doorway, go now, take him by the arm, pull him down, cut out the mole, split the hair, smash the brain, smother him. It's your son, do you hear, yes remember a woman you once saw and fancied, got into trouble, as they say, condescended to marry, and afterwards . . .

> He wanted a cause your father Aly, some cause, the Spanish war? Yes it might well have been that one. Anyway he went out one evening, said he was popping down to the local, and never came back. It wasn't until a few weeks later that I found bits of jewellery missing, my fur coat, and the piggy I had kept specially for you.

Berg approached the house. His father draped over the banisters, stared into a pool of vomit. Positively no connection, there can never be any kind of communication between us. But already the ideal has been harboured too long, that paradoxical dilemma one desires to rub, formulate into a gigantic cloud-burst, ride past the sun, driven by one's own power, power unequivocal.

Be detached, the considerate neighbour, do what is expected of you. He dragged the old man up the stairs, at the top he let go. His father moaning sank back against the banisters. Now, just a little push, down you go dear. Who would know, in his drunken state? Poor Nathaniel Berg, we knew him well, always said the booze would get him in the end. The sound of Judith calling out made him stand back. The old man whimpered, a dog whose mistress is cross. Go now, drop at her feet, lick her, lick her there, lick her here, in between, above the hair, sweet-scented nuzzle, rush of spring tides. The door closed. His father shivered. Berg lifted him up, holding him under the arms, pulling him into his own room, where he pushed him on to the bed. How ancient he looks – what age, late fifties, over sixty perhaps, and Judith? Behind the dyed hair, the well-powdered face, difficult to tell, he hadn't been that close, at least not yet. The old man's skin like vegetable matter, the eyes rusty pin heads. Berg undressed him, came to the soiled underwear, torn at the back – three bullet holes – and on the yellow wrinkled skin were the large tattoo marks.

He had them done once you know, just for fun, at least that's what he said. Still if there's one sure identification I suppose you couldn't do better.

Berg slowly traced the lettering with his forefinger EDITH MY LOVE AND JOY; further down: IN MEMORY OF MY BELOVED MOTHER. His eyes strayed up at the bulb swinging above, near, nearer. Pluck out, fill up with flowers, pick the petals off, one by one, lie under the fragrant softness. He became aware of the burnt smell again, invading the room, a smell of flesh. He covered the old man with a blanket, closed the window, though he realised the smell would now last the rest of the night, but if lucky it might be gone by the morning. Perhaps the place across the way is a crematorium?

He squatted by the gas ring and watched the milk simmer – a fly about to fall in. It had been a ghastly mistake bringing the old man into his room, things could have waited until another day. As he hovered over the milk he noticed a brown blur floating about. He scooped the moth out, and pressed it on the edge of the saucer. He settled back against the lumpy cushion, the broken springs, the peeled leather arms. He looked once or twice at his father, whom he thought for a moment was awake, in fact, was watching him, but upon inspecting from closer quarters, only a prostrate body covered the bed, one foot flung from the blanket, now and then jerking, nodding in secret communication with the partition. He heard Judith moving about, the sound of plates, and strange sucking noises – perhaps she licks herself? She wasn't a bad-looking woman really, not his type though. He stirred the milk, and taking a layer of skin off, he put it over the moth in the saucer. She really wasn't bad at all; large breasts were quite a compensation for anything else that might be lacking. He reached for the mirror. If she accepted a man approaching his sixties, what would she reject? He rubbed his unshaved chin, smoothed his hair down, and searched for the clip-on bow tie. Almost suave, certainly giving that added touch, an almost gracious air.

There's definitely something about you Aly, a natural aristocrat, your father was the same, or so he liked to think.

He noticed his father's stained threadbare coat, the socks with holes, and smiling he went out, locked the door, putting the key on the ledge above. It paid to be cautious, wouldn't do if his father suddenly woke up, and flew out. Perhaps I presume too much? He knocked softly on their door, eventually opened by Judith, breathless, flushed and frowning. Berg tried fixing the smile he had played with while clipping the bow tie on, but it drooped into the corners of his mouth, as Judith half closed the door. Could she possibly tell him the right time? She sniffed, looked him up and down, then disappeared, but soon swept back. What was she wearing to make such a rustling sound – leaves stirring in the wind? Sorry I don't know, but it's well past closing time. He noticed her glance down once more, at his uncreased trousers, the shiny knees, the smudges between buttons. You haven't by any chance seen Mr. Berg perhaps down the road? Well now she mentioned it he thought he had, yes it must have been Mr. Berg he'd seen talking to someone in the pub. Her fingers that had played with a button between her breasts, now flew, dived into a thin gold net which encased her yellow bush of hair. The gap between their room and the landing widened. He looked at his feet, the laces of one shoe were undone. He bent and played with the ends. Perhaps she'll cry, fall into my arms, I will soothe, pacify her – and then? He gazed at the closed door, and listened, but heard nothing. He made for his own room, reached for the key, fingered it, went back and knocked on their door again. He heard Judith call out, like a child. The door remained locked. Her voice rose – how women's voices altered to suit the occasion, to gratify their ends. The gap widened. Well what is it this time? Berg stepped back, almost in a bowing attitude. A shilling, oh well you better come in, I'll have a look.

On the threshold of their room, a room draped it seemed entirely in purple velvet, reminiscent of an Egyptian tomb, square and dimly lit. Judith's mouth opened, shut, an overripe melon hanging in mid-air. He entered further.

Squatting furniture – senators in conference. In one corner a large gilt-edged cage in which a budgerigar pecked its feathers, or tapped a silver bell. A Siamese cat stretched, uncurled from a velvet cushion. Heavy Victorian ornaments surrounded the room, and taxidermal creatures stared from their glass houses at the wax flowers and fruit. He heard Judith rustle behind a screen, the ticking of a clock. He edged towards the bed – had the partition moved? Judith appeared, bent over her handbag, straightened up, clasping the two jewelled clips. Flutter of wings startled the cat, its tail quivering – large caterpillar against the side of the couch; owl-eyes searching Berg's, revolving in orbits of fire and water, while Judith handed over a shilling. Now how about a night-cap before turning in Mr. Greb, it is Greb isn't it, or perhaps you fancy something stronger? He pressed the warm coin in his pocket. A cup of hot chocolate would be very welcome. Motioned to the couch, which was covered in cat's fur. Clerical grey pin-striped suit draped over the wardrobe door, a pair of suede shoes leered from under the bed, with a pair of blue fluffy mules. Judith behind the screen again. Berg went over and leaned across the bed. Not a sound, had the bastard meanwhile lost all consciousness, cheated me in fact? I must leave, leave instantly, find out. He scrambled off the bed. Judith peered round. He gestured towards the partition. Left the kettle on, forgot, better see about it, won't be a minute. Pulling his sleeves over the frayed shirt cuffs, he made for the door. The cat sprang, pressed against Berg's legs; eyes yellow spools circling outwards, inwards, narrowing into daggers.

He found the old man heaving over the bed, mounds of vomit on the eiderdown, on the rug. Berg locked the door again. When Judith brought the chocolate he noticed she had changed into a housecoat of shiny black material, rearranged her hair, now no longer bound by the net; her eyes carefully outlined into an oriental effect. He sipped the drink, watching her slowly sip hers. Nasty weather lately. You haven't been here long then? What's your line of business, a hair restorer, how awfully unusual? Berg smiled while Judith blew smoke rings, stroked the cat that spread itself out upon her lap, paws kneading the satin-covered knees. Sebastian's a lovely pussy then, isn't he a dear, he keeps me company you know, though Nathy doesn't really care for Seby. She continued pressing her fingers into the fur, as the creature's back arched; loud purrs vibrated round the room. But then he's got Berty, in fact he takes more notice of that blasted budgie than me sometimes, honestly I could scream, you should see the way he talks to the thing, and when Nathy's not around it never sings, not a single note, fancy having a budgie that can't even sing, let alone talk. The way he pokes his head through, you should see, right into the cage when he's feeding the thing. Do you like animals Mr. Greb? Of course Seby isn't a real cat, he knows everything one says, we have to spell certain words out you know. Seby, Seby, there's my darling, there's my beaufos then.

Folds of Judith's housecoat spread into furrows, breaking away, away from the deep crevice in the middle. Aware of the sickly sweet odour of underarms – grass after rain. He hasn't eaten all day, Nathy's been out, though I bought the best seed, it sulks you know, would you believe a creature that size having feelings? Seby nearly killed it the other day, I can't blame him really. Look at it now, staring like that, positively hates me I'm sure. Berg looked at the bird swaying, tilt its head, sea-stone eyes blinking through the bars. He placed his cup carefully on the imitation Japanese table, searched for a cigarette.

Judith handed him a plastic-crocodile box, he took a tipped cigarette out. I do prefer these don't you Mr. Greb? He waited until she had inhaled, then slowly he allowed the smoke to

23

pour from his nostrils as Judith pouted. She crossed her legs, her housecoat slipped back, a dimple showed, a mole on the side of her knee. Berg moved to the edge of the couch. Well that was very nice, nice milky chocolate, there's nothing better, just the thing before turning in. He stood up. Oh must you go, so soon, why not stay until Nathy's back, keep me and Seby company, does make a change having someone to talk with?

Berg sank back, crossed, uncrossed his legs, stubbed out the half-finished cigarette. The bird fluttered, pecking the bell, or looking into a tiny mirror. Sebastian stirred, tail scythe-swinging Judith's thighs. The partition shook. Berg moved quickly across the room. Judith rustled behind. The cat scratched in its earth box. Shadows of the stuffed animals, an owl, a mouse, a fox's mask. He reached for the handle, felt Judith clasp his arm. Must you go, are you tired then, just a teeny weeny bit tired, why not relax here, just for a little while until he's back? Half turning Berg noticed the partition still vibrating, the cat now perched on the table between the waxen fruit and flowers. He twisted the handle, pressed Judith's fingers, then propelled himself out. Aware of her black-shrouded figure in the doorway, behind her the Dresden shepherds, faded water-coloured pastoral scenes, the shiny television set on steel spikes, the sleek cat that yawned, stretched at his mistress's feet. And in its corner the silent, staring bird. A time ago white roses glimpsed through Sunday-curtained windows, a stuffed parrot or two, a silver-papered bowl on the sill, and a lean cat nuzzling newspaper between dustbins. You looking for comprehension. Apprehension only in the curve of road, the winding crescents; memory of music through half-open doors, the corner of a face, key-board, clandestine; Edith's patent shoes, waiting for their tap, beaks avoiding cracks and stones. Blades of light through lace curtains throwing other dimensions out of place. Can one compare a landscape that remains, though the evolutionary surfaces suffer unlimited contradictions? He stretched for the key. Goodnight Mr. Greb pleasant dreams, sleep tight don't let the bugs bite.

If they do give 'em a skite – goodnight goodnight my darling boy sleep tight.

His own room in comparison an ante-chamber, though he looked at the peeled leather chair almost with relief. He threw off the blankets, and stared at the tattoo marks that leaped out from the surrounding grey blotting paper. The old man rolled completely over, then back again, blinking up. What's happened, where am I, what's the time? In a bad way, brought him here, didn't think he was in a fit state to – well to . . . Berg jerked his head at the partition, winking. His father frowned, then grinned, and rolling off the bed he started dressing. Well thanks a lot old chap, you obviously know what women are like eh? Buttoning, zipping himself, struggling into his jacket. Berg helped him on with his coat. Thanks a lot, if there's anything I can do in return just let me know won't you? Maybe we'll have a booze up sometime eh? Oh dear what a mess, frightfully sorry, my dear chap here let me help clean it up, oh I say that's jolly decent of you, terribly sorry, anything I can do in return, just let me know. Thanks again, most grateful. Berg bowing opened the door.

After he had wiped the eiderdown, the floor, the rug, when the house seemed quieter, darker, he lay down and pressed himself against the partition, listening to the sea hissing in the distance.

The partition swayed: a boat without sails, anchored to a rock, yet revolving outside its own circumference. I an albatross, never to fly in a direction taken a million times before. Berg looked at the crack in the ceiling. Follow on the dream, the beginning conjured up in a single second, an isolated thought hooked out of the mainstream of chance. Though now in the cool light of day that grafted itself so firmly, there seemed every conceivable danger, in the approach, the act, the after effects. What better chance than last night, yet it had been thrown away – a second-hand piece of clothing. But I have to feel certain, absolutely sure I have everything under control, that nothing is intruding. How his head ached this morning, as though many fingers poked amongst the tissues, blood and bones. I must recall the precise feelings that have nurtured the present circumstances, when nothing at all from outside interfered, not even thoughts of time past, present, or time future, when doubts of my own reality have dwindled away. Isn't there a moment caught between two moods, that space within, separated from life, as well as death, when the sun is faced without blinking, when eternity lies here inside; no division whatsoever, simply a series of circular motivations? But these hands with their veins from a leaf, there is no separation, only a distasteful similarity. Why though search for proof? Surely I'm no philosopher to analyse the value of reality as opposed to idea, and what is gained by delving into such linguistic labyrinths? Definitely the supreme action is to dispose of the mind, bring reality into something vital, felt, seen, even smelt. A man of action conquering all. The partition jerked again. Berg quickly dressed. Once outside the bracing sea air cooled him down. He watched the waves strike the breakwaters, the pebbles grind against the pier's iron grids. It was too early for many people to be abroad – space enough to breathe, think more clearly, calmly. He'd 'phone Judith, persuade her to come out, on the pretext of a destined clandestine affair. Yes that's all that's necessary, he felt sure, to play on her presumption, her emotional ambitiousness. For him she would be the perfect revenge. What in heaven's name did she see in the old man anyway, it would almost be worthwhile finding out their exact relationship, the real situation between them before going any further.

In the telephone kiosk he fingered the receiver while squinting into the mirror. The close resemblance to the old man made him nearly drop the telephone; the shape of eyes, mouth undoubtedly the same. Only thirty years younger, putting pennies in the box, listening to a cat purring between the dozen blocks. Soon he recognised the landlady's voice scratching the other end, presumably fastening the inevitable safety pin at the top of her blue and white kimono. Goldstein? No she's out, definitely gone, I saw them both leave just this minute. He made a face in the mirror as the purring began again.

Back along the Front, he passed a boy fishing. Any caught? sullen response. Understandable: twenty years back, truant the only release from scheduled days, the caning afterwards a small forfeit to undergo; the jaunt through woods, trout fishing, tadpole catching, and later on in the season, blackberry picking, scrubbed down shyly by Edith, who had a permanent blackberry patch – hidden. Watching through a crack in the door, were other women the same? Babies come out of the breasts. No they don't, I know, they cut's 'em open near the navel, I know 'cos my sister's got a scar there. Don't be silly they comes where they piss. Confirmed, convinced, until a handy illustrated book, torn from cover to cover, followed by girl-in-the-town boastings, experiencing every position, until he felt sick, and aware of an urge to destroy something.

> Never get a girl into trouble Aly will you, if your father was still with us he'd soon tell you, it's not worth it Aly, I know.

What did she know, when she looked so pale, eyes dimming, you almost an enemy for a moment?

Shadow that over-ruled cracks in the pavements, a distorted double face in the windows. Hovering in front of notice boards, scribbled messages, subtle to the degree of disconcertion, or were they only too blatant for others? Would rubber wear be fitted purely personally by Gloria? Could flute lessons possibly be worth a guinea an hour – the French method? If only he had some more pennies, a velveteen voice would perhaps supply the answer to big and small problems. He peered at the more obvious: rooms ideal for bachelors, a dozen corridor rooms filled with seaweed – suspenders from another age – ready for popping by bald-headed weekenders, serviced twice daily; smooth tightly sheaved sirens sidling along channels of anticipation. But this was hopeless, far worse being the border-line case, brewing on tit-bits made up from the antidotes of artificial respiration upon the imagination; the survival of those who preferred remaining halfway, never accepting, or rejecting, aware only of the urge to defeat boredom. I take, I see, I subject my own mediocre self into something big. Berg walked away from the reflection that threw a superficial slant on the growth that had formed inside.

Soon the morning rush hour, as though the sea itself, swept him down the street to the bus stop, if his arms had not been out he might well have been carried on to the bus. He travelled back slowly, avoiding the sagging leaves, only watching those that were Chinese lanterns swinging above.

Round the corner: an insect flattened against the wall: his father. Berg dived into a doorway, just as Judith click clicked down the street, her hair flying above a large circular fur collar. Had she seen him? At first he thought so. He sidled out, lifted his hand, but she took his father by the arm, and marched away.

A cat brushed Berg's legs; round eyes that narrowed, it began howling, dribbles of brown appeared on the pavement, as the animal half crouched, its tail quivering. Berg lifted his foot. The cat, oblivious, continued shitting, howling. He stretched his hand out, the creature snarled, yellow fangs bared, and still crouching it started backing. Suddenly it sprang, hanging sloth-like on Berg's arm. He caught hold of its tail, and began swinging the cat out, hardly aware of the thud the creature made as it hit the wall. Only later he heard the cries, the howls. A limp body, twitching at his feet. Berg looked round, wondering if anyone had noticed the episode, the street appeared fortunately to be deserted. He picked the body up, threw it in the gutter. While wiping his hands he noticed how shredded they were, the blood stained his sleeves as well as his shirt-cuffs, with bits of fur clinging to them. He walked quickly away.

The wind had risen, carrying the spray inland. Berg pressed his hat down, collar up as he approached the Front. His hands numb; a great longing to press them between Judith's breasts – what and be confronted with an image of the old man imprinted there, perhaps he had a fetish for tattooing his women also, how was he to know Edith didn't have the old man's brand somewhere on her body?

By the water's edge he watched some children digging holes. By a breakwater he smoked into spray and fog that gradually swept the whole Front and shore into obscurity, even the pier could not be seen. The children's voices muffled by the sea, and a few gulls – limp flags – hovered over the breakwater. He must go back soon, enter their room, catch the old man by himself, one blow, that's all that's necessary, or a tight grasp round the neck, that stringy sinewy flesh, wring like one would a chicken, and the remains? a corpse riddled with flies, stretched out on the top floor of a house already rotting with too many ideals. If I could trace a single line below the surface of my assumptions, would there come a point when clarity supersedes the chaos of what has been? The tragic sense of destiny is inherent in every man; but I defy fate, I alone am responsible for every action, every scene; in my nothingness I will create the idea, I shall see what I have imagined, and from that alone will spring my entire actions.

He felt the sweat mixed with spray slide under his collar. Why should it come to this, an isolated day when thought is nearly as heavy as feeling, but if there's illumination in the leaves, why not certitude in knowing, without proof, without the need of tangibility? He pressed against the break-water, arms spread out, a monumental bird worn down by elemental forces. If I simply say 'I am', or 'I love', these are hardly enough, not even the most indulgent of all actions 'I shall kill' can make me declare 'I am' therefore God is. Why the power, the grace of being a god momentarily, surely one can gain this state for longer? He watched a gull circle above until the mist gathered it away. I want – what did he want this weedy, carrot-headed individual – rusty, old rusty, your Mother's washed your hair and forgot to dry it – who had never loved, or been loved, outside the restricted gratification of fornication? He turned over, and lay on his back, watching an insect move into a crack in the stone work. I want to embrace not a woman, nothing so contradictory, but to weigh all values, true or false, and plunge straight on, wallow if need be, define the connection, heal once and for all the dream-ends with reality.

Other days by the sea in a 'kiss-me' hat, candy-floss fingers grasping Edith's scrubbed hands; why does the sea move, what makes it move, did Jesus really walk on the water? Why can't I walk on the waves too? Running, always running away, but scurrying back, wondering if the sun would be pulled out again; the swish swishing of the green-eyed monster rolling under the palace floor and the demons crying from their fortresses that guarded the sun, whenever you were on holiday by the sea; buttoned up in plastic mac and hood, sipping tea in the pavilion, while pinheaded men played violins, and old ladies coyly reclined their blue-tinted heads giving their crumbs to Pekineses.

He walked back along the deserted beach. The sea merged into the mist, vague shapes inland. He stumbled against some steps, a few strands of seaweed wrapped round his legs, and something like wet fur brushed against his face. He climbed the steps and followed the four-headed global lights of buses that trailed like heavy robes through the streets.

Slightly dazed he entered a cafe, ordered tea, cigarettes. He blinked at the table cloth squares, noting the stains made by those he was akin to, yet destined never to share his life with. He licked the scratches on his hands, pressed them firmly on the cloth, a stain soon distinguished from the others. He ordered three cakes, ate two, and half-finished the tea.

Was that Judith disappearing round the corner? He followed, until reaching the pier a stranger's whalebone face looked suspiciously at him. He walked by with a superior air, but his stomach rolled somewhere between the iron grilles, and the lapping of rough tongues far below. He leaned over, scanning the cliffs, the shore, the façade of off-white lodging houses, the hotels, all discarded props, that could be seen now as the mist lifted.

But why there Aly, of all places, why should your father be there, and why must you go now looking for him, can't you at least wait until the weather's warmer?

What could he say, how much could he tell Edith without causing offence, corrupting her vision of the past? Yet shouldn't she know, more than anyone else, she should surely understand? In a wood the happy family trio.

Off you go Aly be a good boy now and pick Daddy and me some flowers, look for some of those nuts you found last year. Why not find some birds' eggs while you're about it?

While they turned their backs you scaled a silver tower, swayed on an oaken throne, spying on the antics of a woman and man you promised there and then to disown. Her voice gently chiding, until gradually raised – a creature trapped – his cooing and the movement back and forth on the grass, weaving of arms, legs scissor-opening. Nearby a startled thrush left seven eggs. You clinging to the bars above, breaking them one by one, throwing six eggs on to the dry moss. Through the keyhole afterwards, in the long dark hours, when you dared not look any more – the sap that creeps from wood on fire. Do you want anything sir? By a kiosk, staring at a chalked face, surrounded by masks, balloons, sticks of candy-striped rock. Berg left the pier, and walked into the park, trailing through corn-flaked leaves, trying to be – feel anonymous. What does one do in the morning of a weekday, off-season too? No au pairs to flirt with, or expectant mothers basking in the sunshine to smile secretly with; no school-girls to encourage in playing truant; far too cold to sit by the fountain and read the news, watch the cocking dogs, or listen to the children's laughter.

He walked once round under the trees, until the pale sun became paler, and the hum of traffic, sounding like Atlantic breakers, drove him into a news-theatre, where he masturbated during the adverts, and in the intervals followed the spotlight on to the white-uniformed blonde usherette. He bought an ice cream, some peanuts; slowly licking the chocolate off the ice, he screwed the wrapper up and pushed it down the side of the seat in front.

He emerged: eyes, nose, ears corroded with smoke, condensed heating, the smell of fish and chips, into the multiplying noise of a town bent on reminding that this is a super civilised hygienic century, tomorrow you may die, but today you live and make merry on instant blood pumped through processed robots that make daily headlines trivial. That's it sir apply twice nightly, smile, wide, wider smile, bottle produced, liquid over fingers, traced across the scalp, the sale's yours.

Hair tonic of course it's in Aly old chap, what with all this fall out, they'll be needing it sooner or later. Yes I dare say for short hair too, you can't go wrong can you?

A genuine guarantee, only tonic on the market that proves its value and yours at the same time. Buy Berg's and be a man, you'll not regret it . . .

But there's no superannuation Aly, and what about a pension at the end, you haven't thought of that have you now?

Why with a smile like yours old chap you could sell 'em porno paperbacks and they'd think they were buying Snow White.

But weren't most people aware of their inferior position, situation, role in life, didn't they all sooner or later assume a negative attitude, the other side of the grave – two feet in, one hand out? This time it means a leap, if I pursue the idea, lay it out before me for much longer it could so easily collapse. It means, of course, supreme action.

As he approached the house everything appeared almost without concrete formation; the dance hall, church, houses all flat shapes. At the same time he became aware of every muscle straining forward, each finger tingled with blood; conscious even of the grey hairs, the dirt between toes, the wart near his navel, the mole under his left arm. Everything is possible – a flower after a long dry spell opening up, receiving rain. On the landing he heard Judith and the old man talking. He edged nearer their door, looked through the keyhole. He saw his father swinging a bottle, every now and again taking huge gulps. Judith, half naked, sprawled on the couch. He knocked, stood back. Silence. He looked again, both of them were transfixed, glaring at the door, at each other. He knocked again, and yet again. Still no answer. Kick the door down, with two shoves the old man would be through the window. And Judith? He heard the budgerigar singing. He whistled, the bird stopped, he almost saw the tilt of its head, beady eyes through the rusty bars, their faces raised, mouths open, eyes fixed on the door. He entered his room, knelt on the bed. He heard their voices, low now; what were they saying, discussing, planning? If only he could make a hole in the partition, just large enough for his eye. He fingered the wood, felt it respond. He searched for his penknife, and started scraping, but the noise alone made him pause, besides the wood was far too solid, it needed drilling. Anyway he wasn't that interested in what went on between them. The only thing that consumed him would soon be over. He lit a cigarette, inhaled slowly, and lay back. Beyond the crack in the ceiling the old man's face, besotted, blue: an under-water plant billowed out, eyes gleaming, ready for plucking; a final gesture to the claims, and counter claims of hereditary. But I don't belong to anyone, therefore attachment to anything means betrayal, self-banishment, renounce self-continuity, self-transcendence; the ego only there to give significance.

The partition began moving, and at one point he thought it would give way altogether. He buried his head in the pillow, which had a lingering moth-ball smell, mixed with stale tobacco. But there were eyes surrounding him, from the sea, serpents that flicked their tails in the iris, reflecting the prismatic colour of the dance hall lights. If I could only make things bow before the majesty of complete omnipotence, draw a halo round all desires. Why does power always escape as soon as touched? Is it all that necessary to have minions down the line carrying out orders, to succeed and shed responsibility by denying oneself the extreme point of action? ACTION! Even now he was dragging on to the skin that covered the growth; I must tear apart, bring it into sight, why hesitate any more?

The best opportunity would be when his father was drunk one evening. Yes wait until then, meanwhile, maybe a perfect alibi should be worked out, for the perfect crime? No, no, hardly that, a slight mistake over the margin either way, so easy to make a mess of things, one small slip, something overlooked. Remember nothing, as yet, has been accomplished anywhere near perfection. Consider, reconsider well beforehand, every point, down to the minutest detail, mark out all the angles.

He traced a geometrical diagram on the peeling wall behind the bed. Strategy definitely is needed, thought before action; hopeless to do anything in the heat of the moment. Flaked pieces of distemper fell on his head – snow upon a ploughed field – he closed his eyes. Why should I ultimately fail, climb up only to fall? Speculation in the absurd surely sets limitations on the very axiom of the project? March ahead, unafraid. He turned his back against the rain that spluttered on the window, and buried his face in the pillow, away from the burnt smell that had this time decided to remain for the night, for the day.

Two days since the old man had left. Berg listened to Judith pattering about behind the partition; her endless trips to the top of the stairs if the telephone rang. Had the old man left for good? Why didn't I follow him when the chance arose? As though the mental effort of calculating the right moment had more or less paralysed me physically. Forty-eight hours, and here I am still; one tin of baked beans remains, one rasher of bacon, that's probably gone bad, and hardly a shilling left for the meter. Should enquiries be made about the old man, without of course causing too much suspicion or curiosity? The landlady could be tackled first. He better come back, do you know Mr. Greb they haven't paid the rent for over three weeks, so if you see the old chap, or her, say I want a word. Put up with a lot of things I do, what with them not even married, still it's none of my business, I mean as long as they keep the place fairly decent, pay the rent. Even so I think she parades herself about too much, no sense of shame these days. I wouldn't go near her if I were you Mr. Greb, don't go knocking her up for a shilling, or anything like that, if you want one then come down here, I've always got plenty. If he's left, well you can't blame him really. Mark you me it won't be long before she sets up with some other poor blighter, I know her type.

Berg grinned into the mirror, at the landscape accustoming itself to the interior planning; pressing his fingers into the furrows on his forehead, around his nose, mouth, then up again, hesitating at the pale perplexity between the creases under his eyes. Wasn't it purely a matter of working on Judith's feelings, on those emotions which have not quite dried in their cast? Who knew the outcome of such an alliance, persuaded in the right way wouldn't he eventually have ample reward?

Should a note be pushed under her door, or better still wait until they met on the stairs, though lately only glimpses had been caught – give it time. Time? Even now someone passed by outside, was it Judith? Berg opened his door a little, saw his father peering through the keyhole next door. So the bastard's returned – no, wait a minute, no, hell he's turning away, but why? Had he just come back on the off chance, hoping Judith wouldn't be in, collect belongings, leave for good? Already the slamming of the front door.

Berg could not see his father in the street. He walked on, until he reached the outskirts of the town. The sea a monster that turned over in a drugged sleep. Rain brushed his face. Sheltering in a subway he heard the sea as through a shell. At the end of the tunnel the light expanded into a huge white fish then it shrivelled. Christ what luck, incredible fantastic piece of luck, the gods are surely with me. The old man weaving down, now nearer, now two hundred yards away. Berg flat against the wall. The pounding of the sea in his ears. Well, well fancy seeing you old chap, what foul weather eh, out for a stroll? Damned rain, soaked all my fags. Oh thanks old man, you smoke these too, not bad are they, got a light on you? A hand produced, the shrunken head poppy-nodding one yard away; pin him down, now, now. Actually you're just the person I wanted to see. Teeth that clicked, the sort that grind in the night; haven't I heard them seven nights from the other side? The ticking of an antiquated watch, now ticking against the bastard's metallic heart. You see, well it's rather a tricky situation, but I feel sure you'll understand. I've decided to leave that place, I honestly can't go on, she's mad, obviously quite nuts, I should have left ages ago, but you know how it is; well the final straw was when she found her bloody cat down the road, blamed me, yes me, for killing it, or if not actually violating the damned creature, it was my fault for leaving the door open, I ask you, me, who wouldn't look the howling dribbling creature in the eye, so it came to a head, in the middle of the night too, she suddenly pounced on me, hit me black and blue, I can show you the bruises if you don't believe me, and all because of that bloody cat, well I couldn't stand it. Now the problem is old chap, my budgie is there and in mortal danger too unless I somehow get him out. The thing is I thought if I gave you the room key you could pop in, when she's out of course, and retrieve Berty, and also, if you wouldn't mind, collect a few things, shirts and so on, I've made a list on this bit of paper, you'll see I've put down where they can all be found. And there's also a ventriloquist's dummy, actually he's most important, in the wardrobe, at the back, I think on the left side. You see I'm going on tour with a friend, a sort of vaudeville act, hope to make a bit of lolly, doing the resorts as soon as the season begins. Thanks a lot you're a pal. I'm staying at the Seaview hotel, you know, opposite the pier, the side-turning, so any time this week, she's sure to go out sometime before Friday.

They parted by the pier, shaking hands, smiling. Berg fingered the key, while watching his father weave towards the hotel. He crossed over, screwing the list up. He entered a supermarket and bought a tin of beans, several bars of chocolate, and a frozen pie. Recalling Edith's plum puddings, her rosy, yet frail face above the round table, framed by a window, a doorway, or above the bed; delicacies when ill, the rubbing of chest and back. Folds in the curtain, division in the head; fold over and above, then under, separating the past from now.

He cooked the beans and the bacon, until the steam curled over the window and mirror, while the moisture thickened on the walls. He sat on the edge of the bed, and balanced the plate on his knees, musing between each mouthful. Of course it's ridiculous to think the whole thing is simply a vehicle for revenge, or even resentment – hardly can it be called personal, not now, indeed I have never felt so objective. If inherent in the age, well and good, though historically speaking the idea perhaps is a little decadent. What am I precisely hoping to prove – to jump in one clear bound from a tight rope strung between invisible walls, enclosed on all sides, and would there be unconditional space afterwards, that's to say if everything went according to plan? It's nothing but a crazy insect that's been half-bitten, now wriggling itself out of an unwanted skin. Perhaps it would have been easier to have come to terms with it – all very well turning in on the point, nourishing the desire over years of frustration, but what if one doesn't ever accept or reject in the end, the accusation in Edith's eyes, the corner of her mouth turned down have to be faced. Berg held the fork up watching the light – an Egyptian queen that danced, imprisoned in a silver tower – he stared at his reflection in the plate, a faint glimmer of someone barely recognisable. Another class, born in a different environment, who could say what the outcome? Surely a matter of luck whether one is swaddled in silk or cotton, and besides who was he to blame for what had gone before? I, the undersigned, hereby swear to be condemned by one that holds no other name but Alistair Charles Humphrey Berg. Why allow an outsider to destroy something that will grow from now on only when it chooses. Haven't I secretly despised, scorned those who have either caressed or kicked me; why put up with the abortive attempts at grafting me to their ideas and ways? Admittedly I have complied up to a point, but there's always been the contempt, the nausea, though hardly recognised as such at the beginning.

I don't understand you Aly, honestly I don't, none of us can make you out at times, what is it you want, what do you think life owes you?

But he could hardly expect Lotte and all the other cousins to touch him now. At nine, at thirteen, even eighteen years yes he cared, cared to the point of becoming dumb in their company. They never touched that crucial centre, he could at least hug that to himself; not even Lotte with tits like hers and eyes cast from a furnace.

Your father was the same, always great plans for the future. This is it he'd say, really it's going to be all right, bring us in no end of profit. Five hundred quid's all I need, cousin Murry's spoken to the chap, and we'll soon be all set up, opening at the end of the month, that's if we get the money of course, all we require is a sponsor. Well there he was with a borrowed hundred at the dogs, of course he'd lose the lot.

Was he any different fundamentally, surely like most, right from Neolithic man, he longed only to be judged as someone worthy of receiving all due rewards, the feast of the gods, as it were, without necessarily giving up his soul? If he couldn't be a god, or come to terms with those who ruled, then the images would have to be destroyed.

Berg scratched his wrists, four fingers that meant nothing to him in that moment, an action performed regardless of conscious thought; desire caused half an hour before perhaps, with the space of light years, how many times would the desire be followed by coldblooded action? Defeat the desire and act. He shaved, feeling his way over the grit-like surface. Yes, that's what it amounts to, decide rather than desire. He shook the lather into the basin, watching the drops like snow slide down, disappear into the round dark mouth. He placed the razor against his neck – not there you fool, the wrists, the wrists. Someone knocked on the door, he put the razor on the edge of the basin, wiped his face, and smoothed his hair down.

Judith, sleek, shiny in blue and gold. Thought you might like to pop in for a little while, have a look at tele, you're all on your own, and so am I, won't you Mr. Greb. Will you, won't you said the . . .

He sat once more on the velvet-covered couch, with its lumps of cat's fur still clinging round the sides. A waiting room can hardly compare, a corner of a room her smile, the blue orange fangs of the gas fire, the flickering of the television. His hands fumbled down the side of the couch. His shoulders hunched. I've got cramp in the right knee, oh dear, no it's all right stay where you are Mr. Greb, it often gets me, bad circulation that's all. He leaned further to his left. Her knee, her thigh, her cheap but overwhelming scent like incense, and behind her an owl stared out from the glass case with its glassy eyes. Berg's hand – a mouse – crept over. Not here, not now you fool. Incredible the inopportune moments that are apples falling in the dark, pick them up and someone inevitably sees, shouts out. There it's gone, funny how something like that can cause you such agony. Oh do look isn't she lovely what a beautiful cat – oh Mr. Greb I forgot to tell you about poor Seby, passed away, run over down the road, Nathy left the door open, the fool, and she must have followed us out, poor thing, quite broken my heart. Berg nodded, sighed, and plucked a few stray bits of fur from the sofa, pushed them down the back. I didn't like to say Mr. Greb – I mean Aly may I call you Aly we are neighbours after all, you can call me Judy, yes, yes, I insist. Well you see he's left, we had a little tiff, you know how it is, he went off in a huff, not come back since, he's done it before, and comes back after a day or so, oh I know it's been two days now, but I'm not worried really, he can well look after himself, he'll be back as soon as he needs me, or a clean shirt, or his darling Berty. She laughed, nodded at the cage, now on the floor, covered up, in the corner. Berg looked back at the blue-bound bosom with its glittering dragon pinned in the middle. She's not unlike a display dummy really, the one that's left in the window at the end of a sale; lips expressing colder winters, colder thoughts; creases in her forehead, lines and circles that told their own stories of frustration and indulgence. Edith's face once in a lift to the underground, her small body upright, her tiny bony hand clutching his arm, Pressing close, shrinking into a frailty he secretly loathed. Nothing here to remind of what was once so important. There it's over, quite enjoyed that, didn't you, switch it off Aly, left knob towards the right. How about a drink, call in up the road shall we? Berg watched her bend, the split of her skirt wide, as she straightened her stocking seams. He stood up while she wriggled into her coat.

She hung upon his arm, chattering still, about this and that. He noticed half her eyelashes had unpeeled – spiders' legs hanging over the edge. The pub full; faces turned, in mid-conversation, hesitating over their drinks as Judith sidled her way through into the Saloon bar. They sat either side of a glass-topped table, above them a cherub-garlanded mirror, into which Berg gazed at the blind man thumping the piano, the flushed businessmen's faces, and Judith's, her mouth con- tinually yawning, her eyes flickering over everyone, eyes that came to rest on someone just entering. It's him Aly, would you believe it, he's seen us too, pretending he hasn't, just look at him, gone right past into the other bar, what does he think he's playing at, Aly did you hear me, did you see him? He watched her face grow crimson, her eyes a rabbit's trapped. Look you stay here, I won't be a minute, just want to pop round to the ladies. He watched her push her way through into the public bar. In the mirror he saw two women emerge from the toilet upstairs. He looked clairvoyantly into his glass. Counsel for the defence, I put to you, does the guilt lie in ourselves as others see us? Action alone gives you away; what I think, what I may dream can cause no alarm, no fear either side. But this, her words, surely out of context, anxiety on her face as she walked away – scattered pollen covering a dry patch of uncultivated ground. Outside the air strong; the sea a huge machine churning over the town. Berg walked down to the beach, and sheltered behind a boat. Here he smoked, watching a couple make love under the pier, watching the manoeuvring of their limbs, as though they were assorted feelers searching for a hiding place. The girl's slight resist- ance for the pleasure of the final surrender, the momentary security of the victim. Berg stared at the pebbles, picked two large ones up, threw them towards the sea. He heard the girl giggling, the man murmur. He threw three more pebbles, only the last one hit the water. He leaned against the boat, his eyes closed, feeling the salt from the spray already in his mouth, and a few grains of sand in his eyes. Smell of seaweed together with oil and tar drifted by him. He waited until the couple had gone before walking back. Past the huddled shapes of tramps moulded into their lumps of rags and newspaper, twitching and squirming under the pier.

Climbing the stairs; walls like the formation of rock – scale, bore a hole at the top, large enough for the head, space enough to breathe. He kicked his door open, and fell into a beam of light from the dance hall. But tonight somehow the sight and sound of couples miming the act of love across the way sickened him into drawing the curtains. End of term dances, the village dance, the Saturday night urge, the slow process of sprucing up; polished boots, the farewell kiss.

> Don't be too late Aly, and enjoy yourself, have a good time, here wait a minute you've got some fluff on your nice suit, let me brush you down.

A pint of beer, reclining in a corner, terrified of so much sophistication, everyone that much more adult, more knowledgeable in the rules of the social game. Your shoes squeaking on every turn, the toes pinched, blistered heels for at least a week after; pale acne-face. After two drinks manoeuvring towards some plump piece, only to be too late, or defeated by best friend's giggles. Sliding out before the last waltz, circling the spotlights, with heart lurching somewhere between belly and toes. Back down the garden path, the light in her window, knowing your bed would be warm, the sheets just laundered, ironed by her, the eiderdown rolled back.

Is that you Aly, did you have a nice time, oh well you know I can't sleep until you're back.

Later the refusal to go anywhere, head buried in books, occasionally an outing to the pictures together.

You ought to mix a little more at your age Aly, why don't you join the Club, a nice crowd go down there, even Mrs. Deal's Johnny goes on a Saturday night?

The warmth, in the winter, sitting together by the fire, reading to each other. Then came the army, head shaved, emerging like sheep, the awkward youth into – what though? hardly manhood. Two years of castration, the silent masturbation in lavatories, after lights out. Admittedly you learned how to make contact by spraying a fashionable, acceptable brand of sanctity on to others. Then the decision to take to the road. Tears, followed by martyred resignment; Edith's face dwindling away at the station, and for yourself? The tremendous relief at last in shedding the responsibility of being someone you could never hope to live up to, as though in fact she held a photograph of the old man in front of you and said:

There you see that's your father who left us both, you'll have to do a lot to overcome him Aly before I die.

Had he failed, was he a coward to the end? As from the beginning, from behind those sheltered paths of unrepenting sunfilled days, the miraculous discoveries; patterns of sunlight, shadows, shapes of stones, hills that moved through the dark, when you were filled with a world that was strictly your own. Lying starkers in a wood, under damp, soft warm leaves with their delicious feminine smell. Oh yes you were singing green in a golden age, dancing by the waters' edge, under a mosaic sky; feather-crowned, grass-patterned thighs, and seven-leagued boots, petrified mud, magenta amazed. Birds' eggs for sale, a heart in exchange; sherbet-stained, lolly-pop thumbs, liquorice hair – ringlets up to the age of five, afterwards wrapped in tissue paper, kept in the right-hand side of the chest of drawers in Aunt Flo's room, next to her own, when she was a girl, long black tresses which she fingered with that far away look. Didn't they say if shorn hair is kept that person will always be sick? Were his locks still there, soft and golden? Sunday school, you pressed and polished, straight and starched, bargaining over pictures of the Holy Virgin with snakes coiled round her feet, the transfer stamps all the way up your arms and legs. Secret notes passed behind the pews. Only perhaps now recalling the shaft of light, the summer's half-hearted breezes through the swinging chapel door; the mumbled hymn-singing no one ever really knew; peering through a crack in a grave, in awe at the stick-like bones, or staring at unpronounceable names inscribed on marble, counteracted by own writing on pavements and garden walls: Josie loves Aly; Barney Broadbent stinks. The tree with the swing, the hollyhock bowers; untouchable ladybirds, catching a Manx by its stubby tail; trespassers be warned. But you king of the jungle, a warrior supreme. I see an eye through a slit in the wall, my own unique eye, insouciant at everything, beyond what it can now see.

He unrolled a burnt-out cigarette end, crumbling the tobacco on to the floor. Well over a week spent idling, and worse, he was running out of cash, an overdraft of sixty pounds – how things are there round every corner, waiting to sneer, pounce on one. But use reason, be at least rational about the situation. Surely nothing is lost, not yet. Aren't I miscalculating my own appeal, the two extremes that flatter the maternal instinct in women – the tender and the cynical? But then perhaps the old man is back, this very moment behind the partition – no, no don't think of him, don't think of them there, doing that, and if he is back? Well what's stopping you from ousting him out, after all you have the advantage of being nearer Judith's age, hadn't she more or less suggested by her glances, gestures that you are, could be, a potential lover? Yes he could give her emotional security, and in return? But first let's transfer all this, juxtapose these thoughts and ideals into rational propositions, be rid of the half-formed desires, tyrannical, brittle under a blemished eye. But these hands, are they adequate, capable of producing more than just pity on her part, her thighs, would they open at the slightest provocation – these fingers, now flat, white, uncaressed, a language of their own, what are they really capable of?

If only sleep could release me. Stretching his legs he tried relaxing, first with the toes – this one went to market, and the remaining? He climbed off the bed, swept back the curtains, and watched the tapering fingers from the trees strike a window opposite. Half in the light he stood, a Pirandello hero in search of a scene that might project him from the shadow screen on to which he felt he had allowed himself to be thrown. If I could only discover whether cause and effect lie entirely in my power.

Hearing footsteps in the street, he leaned farther out. He drew back. So. He put his finger through the hole in the top part of their key. Soon he heard Judith giggling, the old man wheezing, as they came up the stairs. He banged the window down, switched the light out, lit a cigarette, and lay back on the bed. Now he heard them the other side. Silence: ten minutes, quarter of an hour, half an hour. God will it never end, what are they doing, or need I think of that? Didn't the partition speak for itself? Something suddenly fell, as though a heavy object had been hurled across the room, hit the bed, bounced against the partition, now their raised voices, followed by the sound of doors opening, closing, steps retreating, stairs creaking. He switched the light on, walked round the bed. Judith had started crying. He tapped on the partition several times; the sobbing continued, with renewed force. He went out, and using their key entered.

Immediately confronted by warmth, smell of wet fur. He lowered his head, but the warmth was no longer there. You, how did you get in, how dare you, get out, do you hear? Men make me sick, what do you want? The light showed him Judith's blotched face, pigeon eyes with mascara fly-squashed in the corners. He swayed between doorway and landing, watching Judith shrink away, finally collapse on the couch, in another fit of weeping. Oh I've lost him for good this time, he'll never come back now. Well I just don't care, do you hear, he can go to hell, and stay there. Look what is it you want for Crissake, oh what shall I do?

Berg advanced, stopped, circled, stared at the fox's mask, fingered some artificial flowers, and peeled a plastic petal off, which had, it seemed, just been washed. Then swiftly he left, quietly closing the door, and jumped the stairs two at a time. Dreaming once I became a star, waiting to disintegrate, gradually breaking apart, splash a rocket across the Milky Way. Always this paramount desire to use up the shell – can the shape of the body be the soul, what outward manifestation ever reveals our innermost feelings? Yet there's enough truth in these steps I take, this cigarette I light, that leaf pressed between a crack in the pavement, and the woman I've just left in tears. But once attached then I begin questioning, making demands. Surrounded by many blocks of flats: square eyes, sewn-up mouths, lopped-off trees, broken glass, and my shadow dribbling round corners.

He made diagonal trails through the leaves, stopping once to stroke a cat, a bushy tiger with azure eyes, half contemplating the idea of taking him back, a present for Judith, but even as he put his hands out, a face appeared, and another's hands grasped the cat. Berg was left staring at the fog that swept up from the sea, lapped over the houses, at the large leaves – bat-like fluttering round leopard-marked trees. He took in air as if risen from the ocean bed, at the same time he threw back his shoulders, ready if need be to bear the full weight of the town.

He paced outside the hotel, hesitating several times in front of the revolving doors before diving through. Mr. N. H. Berg room 301, seventh floor, lift is just over there sir. He squeezed a pimple until the blood spouted out. Along a corridor he padded, confronted by every number except the vital one. Was he perhaps on the wrong floor? Door upon door, separated merely by strips of plaster and pink wallpaper damp-stained; the carpet as though just unrolled leading perhaps to a saw-dust ring. Everywhere the smell of disinfectant.

He stared at the number 301 as if mesmerising each digit, split them in half, add, subtract, multiply. The door opened on to a small circular room, sparsely furnished, though a few familiar objects were scattered about. On the bed: a pair of faded suede shoes, a comb, a clothes brush with worn bristles, several dirty handkerchiefs, a watch and chain, and an imitation pigskin wallet, which was empty. Hearing the sound of water running, Berg went towards a connecting door. Why hallo old chap, fancy seeing you here at this time of night, well, well never mind, take a pew, I won't be a second. I suppose you've brought the things, jolly decent of you I must say. Berg advanced, two, three steps towards the bath. How would anyone ever know, there were, after all, numerous accidents one read about in the daily papers, and accidents in baths were not rare; fill up until overflowing, slipped, knocked unconscious against the taps. I say old man you couldn't switch that on again, water's a bit cold now. Burnt skin sizzled into nothing. The mirror steamed over. I say old chap you've put it on too hot, turn it down there's a good fellow, thanks, that's better. I say you wouldn't mind scrubbing my back, you know how it is never can get round to it . . . Ah that's nice, that's lovely, just a little lower, to the left, ah, oh, that's just right, that's it, just there, no wrong again old chap, a little higher this time, to the left I said, yes that's it. Wait a minute need some more soap, up there on the shelf old sport, yes that's the one, smells good, just what the baby wants eh? Ever heard the joke about the Englishman, Irishman and the Scotsman? Ah well it is rather an old one I suppose, hey what about the one about the woman who went to her doctor and said she had an itch between her toes and he . . . A host of pimples down the spine, the tattoo marks somehow faded under the cloudy water. Fill the bath up a bit more old chap, that's it, hey that's enough, steady on, water will be over the top soon, well as I was saying, this woman had this itch . . .

Metal against moist hands, nothing could be simpler, now, NOW. Here steady old man, nearly had me over then you know. Pass me that towel, that's the one thanks a lot. Here you seem to be bleeding, looks as though a cat's scratched you, or was it an even more feline touch eh Greb? There's some cotton wool in the cupboard, top shelf, that's the job.

Gurgle of water going down: a warden groaning. But he escaped when I wasn't looking, I mean I was hardly prepared. Yes it should have been him, blood and flesh in bits and pieces floating about against the smooth white with the water lapping softly over, ever over. There that's better, all clean and healthy. Now Greb where did you put my things, is Berty all right, have been rather worried about him, didn't have much chance to see him earlier on? Yes I went back, well I thought it might be a good opportunity to collect a few things, but nag, nag, nag – women, once they get their vampire fangs into you – yet they dote on you, I suppose that's their appeal, but my God it's their downfall, always want us to be tied to their bloody strings. What's that, but my dear fellow I thought that was why you had turned up, and I did want a few clean things at least, a shirt or two, and as you can see I've run out of snot rags, oh dear, and there's that dummy too, we start rehearsing on Saturday. Tomorrow then, you promise now, first thing? You see I can't possibly afford to stay on here for more than a week, as it is I shall probably have to move out before they present me with the bill – moonlight flit and all that, dreadful bore. And they charge the earth too, bloody cheek really, they call a place like this Seaview, and look, come over here Greb, just take a look at that will you, I ask you, colossal cheek really, a fire-escape, bang outside my window, though on the other hand it couldn't be better, well I mean for a sudden departure and all that. Oh you're not going old man, stay and have a chat, I won't be turning in just yet? Tell me what do you really think of Judy, I saw you together earlier on in the pub, and I thought oy, oy that's fast work?

Berg watched his father's eyes narrow, heard him give an abrupt laugh that might have been a cough, watched him crawl over the crimson bedspread, collecting brush, comb, dropping the handkerchiefs into a wastepaper basket. She's not bad is she Greb really, I've known her on and off for quite a few years now, she accepts my shortcomings, enjoys certain things I like doing, you know what I mean, and one doesn't come across that sort of woman every day, she'd be all right if it wasn't for her rather selfish ways; I mean as regards my independence, perhaps she ought to have children, that usually calms 'em down. I say you couldn't put the window up a little, it's rather cold now, put the fire on too, oh damn I haven't a shilling, have you old chap? Ah that's better, bring your chair nearer, put your feet up, looking a little queasy, a bit pale, you're all right Greb, I mean you're not ill or anything are you? In retrospect I could mutilate an effigy of him, squeeze into pulp, and then from this shapeless mass a beautiful god-like form might rise up. He pulled the chair across, watched his father crouch for a second in the middle of the bed, then drop down, the blue tattoo marks – a trail of inkfish glimpsed suddenly. By the way what's your first name – Aly isn't it, Alistair I suppose? Funny thing I had a son called that, nice little thing, don't suppose he's so small now though. Well I think I'll turn in now. See you tomorrow, and thanks a lot old fellow, you don't know what it means to me, take care how you carry Berty, the cage is liable to be heavier than you think, and sometimes the door rattles, he gets easily frightened. Berg approached the bed, leaned over, felt his hand limply clasped, saw the skin on his father's third finger had been bitten into. Well cheers old man, pleasant dreams, sleep tight, don't let the bugs bite!

He faced the corridor, the endless stretch of pink carpet, the box-like lift, the spinning glass doors that caught and spun the pier lights, the sky that curved towards the sea as the waves swept up the shore.

Let the darkness enter, cover the whole, embalmed, mummi-
fied, only a carcass revealed while I pluck the bones. They're
waiting, the birds, outside to tear me to shreds. Berg pulled
the blankets over his head. The door rattled. If they can wait
so can I. The door squeaked. Berg leaped up, surveyed the
landing, their closed door. Perhaps I died in the middle of the
night – this for eternity? He snatched the mirror up, peered
anxiously into a distortion that made him quickly turn away.
May as well be dead for who would ever accept a face like
that? He crawled back into the subterfuge of the bedclothes,
burying his face into the deep hollow of the pillow. Gradually
aware of an odour that did not belong to the usual smells;
perhaps a bottle of hair tonic leaked? No it really couldn't be
that. He looked up: Judith, Amazon, framed in the doorway.
Did he know where Mr. Berg might be? He crumbled, shook
with laughter. Know, why should he know where her lover
was, nothing to do with him? But he talked only to a corner of
his pyjamas, the stripes running up to the cord, one pull – be
confronted with something larger than an accusing finger;
like velvet, like corn, segments of sun falling; like velvet it is
Aly – the first one said, why had she left so suddenly? The sun
streamed in, upon the wigs, which like clumps of seaweed
were spread about, the bottles already thick with dust. Berg
slowly dressed, each item of soiled clothing chainmailing

his limbs, part by part, until at last his head sprouted out, a hedgehog, with eyes that darted from left to right. Alistair Berg, alias Greb, commercial traveller, seller of wigs, hair tonic, paranoiac paramour, do you plead guilty? Yes. Guilty of all things the human condition brings; guilty of being too committed; guilty of defending myself; of defrauding others; guilty of love; loving too much, or not enough; guilty of parochial actions, of universal wish-fulfilments; of conscious martyrdom; of unconscious masochism. Idle hours, fingers that meddle. Alistair Charles Humphrey Greb, alias Berg, you are condemned to life imprisonment until such time you may prove yourself worthy of death.

Maybe before, yes definitely before entering this place, perhaps even prior to that fateful day when seeing the photograph of the old man, it had started, the stirring of the insect between throat and heart. But what precisely are you proposing to do now, yes you, a pauper who will soon be living off the National Assistance, digging purple toes into a threadbare rug, eyes avoiding the streaks of grease round the gas ring, the dust on the bottles, the chest of drawers, the cracked enamel pot, the crack that runs from one corner to another where the wallpaper ends in a map of Italy. Did these surroundings add up to anything, had they a separate existence; say I decided to leave, would they mean nothing, absolutely nothing? If I could completely wipe out the man of yesterday. What did others do to eradicate the past? But then he had hardly been on intimate enough terms with anyone to know what they might, or might not do in a similar situation. Besides hadn't he always taken others, himself, for granted, creatures of habit, chained to environment, hereditary complaints and complexes. Had the convolution he was now in merely been transferred – destined to rotate the same way? He sat by the window. The sun now hidden by fistfuls of clouds. I relate myself to that, the dismembered trees, half-broken walls, roofs with slates ready to fall off, and the people below with their masks of indifference, and I am aware of an urge to break through them all. Yet how much easier it would be to carry out orders from a hierarchy. Opposite a poster where the lettering had been broken up into spittle on the board CHRIST DIED FOR YOUR SINS. Isn't it enough to save myself? He pulled the curtains together, shutting away the drizzle that now drifted over the town. Of course that's what is always so unforgiveable, the fact that everything will go on with or without my existence. If one could only have all, like Faust, just for one brief moment of absolute belief, and let whatever happens afterwards take care of itself. A voyage presumably that would take one beyond the precincts of an affluent society, the pipedream of a disenchanted age. He felt the reptile creases in his neck, the sweat running over the cracks in his collar, but he almost welcomed this, for he was once more being carried on a huge cloud towards a rainbow he had promised himself. Naturally enough he had been allowing himself time to think the matter carefully over, that was the explanation, well then now everything had been fixed, tomorrow would see an end to it once and for all. He made some tea, brooding over the tea leaves, finally scooping four out, which he shuffled about, squashed them against the side of the cup. Damn, of course, in all this he had completely forgotten to send his usual weekly letter to Edith, that would mean telegrams, urgent trunk calls, or even her turning up, if he didn't write at once. He found a pen, but no ink; would it be wise asking Judith for some, it would mean facing her questionings, perhaps an outburst of tears, a general demonstration against him – all mankind? He searched the chest of drawers and found a pencil.

Dear Mum,

How are you? Everything here is fine. I've seen my father, but so far haven't revealed who I really am (how Dickensian can one get, and what can I really put – that he's been fucking another woman next door, and probably a dozen others besides over the past fifteen years, is about to go on tour with some friend in a Vaudeville show, trailing a dummy around, that he's in love with a budgie . . . ?) Somehow I think you're better off without him, he seems a bit the worse for wear, not at all like the photograph, or even like the ones you already have of him, and he still hasn't any money, as far as I can make out he's sponging left right and centre.

Thanks for the food parcel, and the new set of underclothes, which as you know I appreciate very much. If you could see your way to sending a few quid it would help until I get straightened out – sales have been somewhat tricky here, but I hope to fix up something by the end of the month. Well that's all for now. I think of you always, still it won't be long now before Christmas, then we can have a nice get-together. Meanwhile – meanwhile – well I'm going to fuck her too . . .

He sucked the top of the pencil, a wet brown fang, and pushed his finger through the paper. How can I ever identify myself with such a person as she accepts? He pushed his fist right through, and leaned against the partition. If I turned perhaps the whole structure inside would rattle like a box of nails? But I'm damned if I'll allow the old bastard to get away with it, with the past. I, the son, have every justification, people will sympathise, might even be considered a hero. Who's to stop, denounce or condemn me anyway, the biggest reality lies in myself? He drew a circle in the mirror and wrote NON OMNIS MORIAR. Gulping the rest of the tea down he put his coat on, but upon opening the door he saw Judith about to go down the stairs. He closed the door and waited by the window. There she goes, tottering on exceptionally high heels down the street, hat clutched by ringed fingers. Where on earth could she be going at such an early hour, to catch her darling Nathy perhaps, or had she already secured someone else? But hardly at this time of day? Still women were such contrary creatures, capable of the most perverse at the most awkward times. Well what was he hanging about for, this surely was the moment he had been waiting for? He fingered their room key, wondering how the place would seem without their presence, yet retaining something of their habits; a background composed of things for reassurance, knick-knacks to fill in the odd gaps between petty rows and worked-up passion.

The room reeked of stale tobacco, drink, cooking and perfume. Clothes covered the chairs, bed, and floor. Obviously Judith had tried on various dresses before deciding upon a suitable battle-dress for the day. Cutlery, plates, cups piled high on the table, some even on top of the glass-domed animals and flowers. The bird cage, still in the corner, covered up. Perhaps he should pacify the old man by at least taking that. He picked the cover off, the budgerigar lay on its side, a yellow puffed-up mound of dry feathers, and brown slits for eyes. He put the cover back; this was adequate enough.

Slowly across the park; I a ghost who walks abroad, a Cheshire smile that grows and grows, and giant hands which will squash everything that refuses to hold the rules and regulations I may assign. He heard the cage door rattle, and noticed people turn their heads as he marched on, cheerfully whistling.

The fire-escape beyond three walls. Seventh floor – about half way up. To get there: one wall to be climbed into a backyard. He heard raised voices from the hotel kitchen, where the steam spread over the windows, for which he was thankful, if only for the illusion that because he saw no one, they were blind to his manoeuvres. About a quarter of the way up the fire-escape he felt dizzy. He propped the cage on a step above, and sat down. The seafront, the pier, and the beach were islands that might float on over the sea, yet each section remaining untouched. Why did the town seem so scattered, worse as though it would any minute disintegrate into flotsam if one dropped down and walked amongst it all? Were those small dark figures who inhabited those islands aware of the same feeling this very minute? He heard the faint strains of a brass band striking up from the promenade, which now and then became drowned by some gulls that circled inland. After finishing a cigarette Berg picked the cage up and began climbing again.

Soon coming to a halt, for there piled one on top of another were several familiar articles outside an open window. The sound of an electric razor warned him that someone was in the room. Moving nearer, having put the cage down, he looked in, and through the half-open connecting door saw his father shaving. Lowering himself into the main room he padded across. I say you gave me a fright old fellow, trouble with these things they make quite a noise and one doesn't realise it. Well where are the things? Outside – outside where? You see I've got to be quick, clearing out this morning. How is he, I mean Berty of course old man, I bet Judy hasn't been feeding him poor little thing? Where did you say you've put him, outside the window – you guessed eh? Oh I see you came up that way, tell me is it easy getting over the wall? Berty, Berty how's my little darling? Gently does it Greb, look you get out and hand the cage over, that's right keep the cover on he gets so frightened bless his little soul. I say do go easy, hey look out. Berg watched the old man's hands grasp the air, his eyes lower, his neck contort, as he heard the rattle of the cage become fainter. Quick let me pass for Crissake Greb, what have you done, what have you done, oh my poor Berty, my poor Berty. Berg watched his father spin down the fire-escape. What was the use of calling out now that his beloved bird was dead anyway, that Judith presumably had strangled the creature days ago.

He climbed back into the room, and fixed up the electric razor. Finishing his shave, he picked up the telephone, ordered some coffee, eggs and bacon. He closed the window, drew the curtains, switched the radio on, and lay on the bed, his fingers plucking at the taffeta eiderdown. Holding a handkerchief to his nose he opened the door and took the tray from a waitress, who seemed on the point of saying something, when Berg closed the door.

He ate the eggs and bacon slowly, relishing each mouthful, sipping the coffee. They had forgotten the sugar; it would be too presumptuous to ring through another order. Someone tapped on the window. Well the bastard can knock to his heart's content. It developed into harder knocking, and he heard the old man's gruff voice. Greb you swine let me in, do you hear, let me in at once. Berg turned the volume of the radio up, but the music couldn't drown the noise that now went on outside. Fearing that someone else might well hear the commotion, Berg opened the window. Most considerate of you I must say old fellow – damn you, you know what you've done, killed the only thing I loved, did you hear Greb, yes killed, murdered the only living creature I had any love or time for. Why he's blubbering, actually crying, real tears either side of the mole. First point to Greb, one away, and soon who knows it would be two at home. The telephone began ringing, Berg looked at his father who stared back. They both looked at the phone, back again at each other, once round the room, then at the door, someone now knocked. Quick Greb open the window for Crissake they'll have a bill as long as their menu, and just as false, colossal cheek these people have, think they own the world, nothing but a consumers' race Greb. Quick pass me that mirror, and those brushes, and while you're about it whip that eiderdown off, never know might come in useful some day. Berg snatched up the things, throwing the brushes over to his father, whirling the eiderdown over his shoulders, he climbed out of the window, holding the mirror up, which reflected the buildings, the fire-escape, the sea.

Arriving in the yard they both looked up as though expecting their pursuers to either be half way down, or at least peering, shouting from the window. No one. They climbed over the wall, Berg carrying the cage, and a bundle made from the eiderdown. They sauntered across the road, leaned over the railings, regaining breath. I say Greb pass me the cage. Look at him, oh look at my poor Berty. I say maybe he's not – perhaps he's just sleeping. Hey Berty, Burlington Berty, tweet, tweet, he's a pretty boy then, come on now, it's your daddy speaking to his little darling. Berg leaned farther over the railings, swaying his head in time to the brass band music, winking at one of the women tambourine players. Greb I think he's a gonner, he's really quite cold. Berg saw his father open the cage door, now hold the bird in cupped hands, and as though he would breathe his own life into the creature brought it to his mouth. Berg looking at the sea made to walk away, but his father called out. Rattle of the cage door. Soon the old man had caught up, he no longer held the bird – had he thrown it away? Hardly, more than likely nestling in his breast pocket – he did, however, still have the cage, fiercely swinging it, the door rattled louder than ever. George will miss him, if you see him Greb, you know the pigeon, they were great friends, very affectionate they were, well if George happens to be outside the house any time you could feed him for me. But look I must bury Berty somewhere. Berg made a violent twist with his hands, his father's face faded into an amber traffic light; pluck out, stamp on him, squash out the eyes, cut away the heart, bury next to wherever he buries the blasted bird. Those eyes that crinkle, the mouth of crepe paper. They stood in front of a flowerbed, whereupon the old man knelt and started scraping back the earth. At that moment Berg saw Judith advancing through the park gates, he put his collar up and became a tree. Oh I thought it was you, recognised your coat Mr. Greb. Such a remarkable one then, mustardseed trailing along the ground. He felt something curl up inside, at her pointed formality in the use of his name – considering well considering . . . Awful weather, so cold, isn't it cold? Nathy could you please tell me what you are doing down there, surely this isn't the time to repent for your almighty sins, Lor' what's he up to then? Berg smiled, touched his hat again, tried imitating Judith's anxious gaze directed at his father, who, as if completely unaware of his audience, went on pushing back more and more earth, until finally he brought the budgerigar out of his pocket and put it gently in the hollow he had made, slowly he covered it over with the earth, then with head still bowed he stood up sighing, his hands fossilised hung at his side. You're both to blame persecuting me like you do, both of you, oh yes I know. I like that, did you hear what he said Mr. Greb accusing us of God knows what, besides what's the song and dance about, it was only a bird, and if it's dead so what? You didn't say that over your bloody cat Judy. Don't you dare to talk of Seby in that way, how vulgar you can be ugh, honestly you make me quite sick. Berg looked away. They were obviously going to have a God-almighty row and he would end up by being bait if he failed to be judge. He mumbled some excuse about an appointment. The old man called out. Turning he saw Judith's ringed fingers fluttering around her head, adjusting the angle of her feathered hat, tucking in the stray bits of plumage. He began walking in yet another direction, this time Judith shouted out. By the way Mr. Greb we're holding a party tonight, call in, bring some friends, booze if you like, just a few fireworks, a bit of fun, do come. He held his hand up, caught a leaf kissed it and threw into the fountain.

He entered a pub where a brassy Mistress Quickly served behind the bar. A conversation in which the questionnaires were as short and sharp as the woman's tongue – a dragonfly that slithered under one fang, and pastry hands deftly seeing to one's needs. You're new round here? Thought so, traveller aren't you? Yes you all have that look, well sort of not really belonging anywhere, rootless I suppose you could call it. He felt the many eyes turn in his direction. He drained his glass, and swept out.

Of course your father was quite a good-looker in those days, fancied himself you know, man about town, and well I must say one could, I suppose, have called ours a whirlwind sort of romance, quite swept me off my feet, and what could a girl do in those days there weren't so many men, I mean real men, to go around. Not that you could really call him handsome, but I never did go in for good-looks, something to be mistrusted I think when a man's really good-looking, besides you never know who's catching his eye next.

Why not write Judith an anonymous letter, giving the true facts, as well as a few false bits added here and there, then step in. Making love to her prior to really getting rid of the old man would surely bring greater satisfaction, indeed he had to admit it, there was the possibility she would not prove so fascinating after his father's death. For the time being masturbation was perhaps better in the mind as well as the body, no commitments, no responsibility; thoughts leaking out with dreams, becoming whole, entire universe made up of myself alone. Another figure has ignored the face of time, mocked at the images strutting along the edge of resignation, never whole-heartedly accepting or rejecting the biological counterparts. How often one plays with a projected fictional love: the image of a Ruth, a Helen, Beatrice, Cleopatra. Woman, the mythical creature who warmly welcomes the part her lover hands her. Very well couldn't Judith be persuaded even if it meant a couple of weeks' effort on his part, with letters, small presents, suggestions for secret meetings? Couldn't he prove to her that life itself owed something to her very existence? What you with a pattern that's already too set, never accomplishing the complete formation, only a shape, shadows of shapes, half tones thrown on a cinnamon wall?

He stood in front of the mirror, clipping the bow tie on. He knew more than saw the reflection of couples dancing opposite, and above them over the roofs rockets splashed into numerous stars, then sprayed out, the remains spluttering into the sea. He gazed for a time at the chair – an old woman bent over, the cushion a squat toad in the middle; the pot a cracked Chink's face. Until laughter, music, from next door, and Judith's voice above the rest roused him. Should he appear now? no, no, far better to wait until the party was well under way, maybe even go for a drink first, best to arrive not too sober. He frowned into the mirror, fingering the bow tie, handling a scarlet one. A knock on the door released him from further confusion.

Judith in velvet, two pink balloons moved against him, he squeezed one until it burst, and Judith screamed, prodding him in the chest. Now now Aly ooooooooooh oh not again, oh you are naughty really you are. He poked the other balloon playfully with his finger, eyes riveted on one part of Judith's ample anatomy. She continued hugging the balloon, pulling him by his sleeve towards the door. His fingers strayed for a second on the soft material of her dress, aware of the patch of ferns two yards away, to creep into, be shielded by, perhaps be given all the answers without necessarily searching for them. He noticed she smiled, that her mouth seemed very near, very wide – large enough to hide my fingers, my hand, large enough to . . . Oh come on Aly, don't be shy, there's plenty of girls in there, and drink too, don't tell me you haven't a taste for either. I've seen that eye of yours.

The furniture, knick-knacks, artificial flowers rearranged, moving between it all were plants, tall, thin, short, fat rubbery plants as though released suddenly from their pots. Two twisted either side of him, sticky, clinging, one bent smothering him until he thought he would collapse, another pulled him back on to the couch; tendrils catching his legs, arms up, until somehow he managed breaking out, landing in the middle of the room on his hands and knees. The ceiling appeared lower than he remembered; the bed nearer than ever to the partition. Around him the plants continued bobbing, twisting about to some music that issued loudly from a tape recorder in the corner. Nearby the old man stood on his head, surrounded by more plants, silky ones that stretched, almost seemed to snap as they bent forwards, backwards, spreading round his father. Berg moved closer, saw the dark hairs sprayed out against the flabby white flesh squashed between trousers and pink-salmon socks; his face puppet-like creased, his body swayed, then crumpled – a paper bag that lay in a heap, while the plants bent over, quivered as though with some secret hot-house pleasure; two gathered him up. Do it again Nathy, come on old chap show us your tricks, show a leg, that's it man, up then, up. Berg saw his father grinning; a grin that could have been a grimace, as the circle closed in, the women ogling, the men with narrow eyes, pressed closer together, until at last the old man was upsidedown. Berg turned away. Judith approached. Aly how about a dance, I'm sure with your fine legs you have a very innate sense of rhythm? He felt her thighs slide against his own. She began jerking to and fro, not in time to the music, but as though to some hidden mechanism between her hips and shoulder blades. His father still balanced on his head, even though the audience had now become somewhat bored, for only a few remained looking on. Well there now wasn't that nice, I knew you could dance, you know something Aly you're quite sensual, yes really, once you get going, there'll be no holding you soon, here have another drink, try this, it's called a summit, vodka with whisky, and a drop of lemon, there now how do you feel after that? Her breath warm, his ear practically enclosed by her breath, down his windpipe, across his spine, separating his ribs. The plants extended, some El Greco like floated out of the room. He scratched the floor where the carpet had been rolled up, while his hands searched for anything that might yield to his insistence. That smell once more – wet fur and confectionery; soft hands that encircled, bent him inwards, separated him from the wall, the partition.

A commotion started as someone pulled out a strange-looking object from the wardrobe. Berg noticed his father wave his arms, rush across the room. Leave that alone, for Crissake do you hear? Judith threw back her head shrieking. It's only his silly old ventriloquist's dummy. here throw it over. The crowd that had gathered round the old man sepa-rated as Judith flung her arms out and caught the dummy. That's it, now Nathy what will you do to have it back eh? Berg watched the old man swerve to the left, to the right, eyes that had become mere grains in the rock-like surface. Judy I swear if you don't hand him back this instant I'll . . . He never finished his threat, Judith scornfully swept by, still laughing, firmly holding the strange-looking rubbery figure by an arm. She opened the window. Look Nathy take your last look at your precious dummy it's going to a far worthier cause. Now shrieking in an almost hysterical fit she flung the figure out. A crowd below had gathered and some leaned from the dance hall windows, watching the bonfires that blazed fiercely in the yards and gardens. Judith leaned farther out. That's right take it, burn it, like the rest, burn it until there's nothing left. Pity we didn't take the suit off, it was after all one of your best Nathy, wasn't it my darling? What on earth's the matter, Lor' you'd think I had murdered someone, stop looking at me like that Nathy, Nathy sweetie what's up? Berg watched the old man sway in the middle of the now almost empty room. You'll regret this Judy I swear it, you shouldn't have done that you know, not that, I made him with my own hands, took me a long time Judy, you'll live to regret what you've done tonight. Wheeling, toppling he went out, clutching a whisky bottle to his mouth. Now's the time, your chance, follow him; the perfect alibi – anything could happen; trampled on by the crowd outside, pushed accidentally into a fire, cause for suicide – balance of the mind disturbed, there were witnesses, Judith would testify. Anything could happen in such a state at such a time. Judith's hands encircled Berg's neck. What a state to get in, honestly Nathy's quite mad, still why should we care Aly, why should we bother about him. Aly kiss me, kiss me now, oh kiss me here, I've been dying for you darling, oh Christ how I want you. Her mouth soft, wet, taking in the lobe of his ear, moving down, hands fumbling his bow tie. He pulled at her dress, saw the huge white lump rise out, pushed his face against it. How can I go further when there are things to be cleared up – when I could . . . He struggled away, tried walking in a straight line towards the door. He heard Judith laugh, calling him back. He went on, from side to side, clutching the banisters. My God what had she put in that drink – something lethal? Ceiling collided with floor – the stairs – but I must go on, this is the only time, if I don't do it now I never will.

Spluttering fireworks, licking of flames that almost made Berg turn back, but soon he found himself caught up in the crowd surging towards a bonfire. Was the old man just the other side? Looked vaguely like him, clutching a bottle. Some youths leaped round the fire pulling Berg with them, their faces bobbed about lit by the flames, like masks, some that were masks grinning against the purple and orange light leaping higher and yet higher, and the screams of children as they jumped over illuminated snakes. He was caught up in a circle nearest the fire, the heat making him nearly lose consciousness. He strained back, but found he was dragged on, round and round; there could be no turning back now, and always the other side, in the very same circle, he thought he recognised the old man. A ragged Guy Fawkes leaned over a stick in the middle of the fire, until that was gradually licked up by the flames, it sizzled, then toppled over. The crowd cheering, gathered speed. Throw that other one in, the one the woman threw down. Berg saw his father, not in the circle at all, but hovering on the fringe, his arms out, head sway-ing almost in a maniacal way from side to side, his mouth open, but if he shouted no one apparently heard. Berg broke away from the circle, made towards the old man. Leave it be, that dummy's mine he's not a bloody Guy do you hear he belongs to me? In a whimpering tone the old man pleaded with several youths who held the dummy between them, obviously preparing to hoist it up on the fire. You bastards, give it back, you can't do this to me, stop it I say, ah there you are Greb, look help for Crissake, help me, it's the only thing I've got left. Do you hear me, stop it you fools, thieves, heathens. Berg ducked behind the laughing stamping circle that had gathered round the old man, at the same time he heard Judith laughing, and looking up through the maze of Catherine wheels he saw her leaning from the window point-ing at his father then at the fire. He worked his way through the jungle of sweating writhing bodies, arms and legs that were giant stalks once more twisting round and above him. At last he managed to clutch hold of the dummy's legs, and he pulled several times until he hugged the thing, while the crowd began laughing, jeering. He clambered over the

debris of streamers and fireworks. Catching the old man's
arm he goose-stepped past the booing crowd. Upon entering
the house he faced the old man. Oh thank God, thank God,
is he all right Greb, a bit the worse for wear round the legs,
some of the rubber's burnt, but that can be patched up, the
bastards, and as for Judy I swear . . . But look here Greb you
all right old chap, you look a bit pale, and you're shaking,
here have some of this, need it after that lot out there. The
whisky bottle handed over, cold glass against moist hands.
Berg brought it to his mouth, watching his father adjust
the dummy's pin-striped suit. Coolness becoming fire. The
door burst open, faces thrust in, uprooted mushrooms; a
familiar voice cooing from above. Aly, sweetie, is that you
Aly love why don't you come on up? He looked round: the
old man once more draped over the banisters. He picked him
up. How light he seemed, incredibly so. But this time once
in his room definitely this time it would be accomplished.
What matter if there were voices and faces all round, once
up the stairs in his room, behind the closed door, he could
begin, even the smell of burning mixed with wet fur could
not deter him, not now.

At last I can rest in peace amen. Accomplished. There he is down there, beside the bed, rolled up in the rug, with the eiderdown spread over him. I won't look yet, give me time, just a matter of getting used to the idea, that's all it amounts to really. To what extent can a so-called action be believed when the thing in-itself is no longer apparent? But if you unrolled the rug? No, no, let it remain, hide the sores, the strangulation marks, the tattoo stains, the place where there must be blood. Give me the sepulchre of resilience, when I can nurture the worms that will grow wings, fly to any destination I, their king, might bid them go. How easy it is enlarging upon the whole scene, how much more one gains after the experience! The action, last night's scene, let it take on a gradual formation. Hands, yes your own hands round his neck, pressing into the flabby flesh, and now, even now I can feel the corpuscles of blood slide across my fingers; well wasn't there blood, yes surely a spot or two? Berg peered at the eiderdown. Yes underneath that, and under the rug there would be dry blood. At last action has supplanted idea and imagery; the imbroglio can be finally sorted out.

Admittedly I would never have had the courage, well own up, yes I know, if it hadn't been for the drink. But I wasn't drunk, don't think that, not one bit, I mean I can remember everything, every detail – though he didn't shout, not a sound,

pity really, he was of course completely unconscious, no doubt
knocked out by the drink. Though there had been a gasp, yes
I remember now, like gas escaping, afterwards – after I had
let go, and the head fell back, the eyes, remember the eyes?
Glass-staring, it had been those you couldn't face, that you
had to cover up. Fortunately no one any the wiser, at any rate
not yet. They hadn't followed, no one had noticed him coming
up the stairs, not even Judith – yet hadn't she been calling?
How vague that seemed now, she certainly hadn't been waiting at the top, nor had he been aware of any movement the
other side. She would be the first to call, enquire where Mr.
Berg is – Mr. Berg indeed, yes here I am, ready for the taking
any time, and don't deny you haven't desired me, dreamt of
me; I know, don't I know the shaking of that partition, even
when he wasn't with you, then those tears which are only
an orgasm of the eyes, those fingers you automatically put
into place, you realise they are mine, always mine, do you
hear? Berg jumped off the bed, felt the cold linoleum, toes
curling away from the eiderdown – that oblong lump so still
underneath. He touched a corner of the taffeta material as
though he would pull it off, but stepping aside he put the
kettle on, also the radio. He pushed the window slightly up,
drawing a funny face between the leaf-like frost marks on
the pane, and heard the homely rattle of milk cans, a train
in the distance, buses purring; the quick patter of those
already more than half way through the weekly ritual. How
separated from it all he felt, how unique too, no longer the
understudy, but the central character as it were, in a play of
his own making. And what of you? Yes you down there, you
who will never speak or write a word again, or touch another
woman, rolled up in your moth-eaten covering, how are you
feeling today eh? Are the flames hot, burning hot, have they

singed out your bowels, your tongue, your liver, cut out your heart? Or maybe you are just cold, stone cold in nothingness, emptiness, eternal space.

He sipped some tea, inhaling the steam, his fingers played round the cup's rim, and his thumb went through the opening in the handle. Hearing someone on the stairs he hastened to the other side of the room, and pushed the eiderdown with its contents under the bed. Someone had definitely stopped right outside his door; had they come already for the corpse? Of course not how could they possibly know, he was really quite safe, no one had an inkling. What motive was there, and after all his real identity had never been revealed? Absolutely safe, not even Judith could be aware of a putrescent body lying within a few yards from her bed separated merely by a piece of wood. Whoever it was they moved on. He heard Judith's voice followed by – but that's impossible, when he's here, and yet? Of course not, it's just someone who has remained after the party, yes that was it. But that familiar intake of breath, the grinding of teeth, the wheezing between sentences. If only he could see into their room. He tried piercing a hole in the partition with a penknife – how futile it was; besides wasn't there enough evidence under the bed? He pulled the knife away, with it came a splinter of wood, the partition shuddered – an animal in pain. He would look at the body right now, no more of this delaying until tomorrow. He groped for the eiderdown, and tugged until he had pulled the whole bundle from under the bed. Whipping the top covering off he stood over the rug staring down. Of course it could easily have been someone else, in the dark, yourself far from sober, in the general confusion, with all those faces appearing suddenly, the heat from the fires. Had it been all for nothing then, a stranger's body rolled

up in my rug? The eiderdown by the side like the remains
of a landfall. He touched the edge of the rug tentatively,
as if expecting that whatever was inside would jump out.
Didn't it move just then? The hump in the middle, and in the
threadbare strands of the pattern, yes right there, weren't
they eyes, two cupreous eyes? He flung the eiderdown back
again, and looked round the room; where could he put it,
under the bed again, it seemed the most suitable place, and
yet – under him at night, in the dark, tonight? How long
would it take for the rot to set in, the smell, bad enough
coping with the burnt smell, but that plus . . . well what
did a dead body smell like? Ah you didn't think of that, you
hadn't planned for that Aly. Edith's voice – a wooden spoon
stirring the mixed murmurings in his head.

What will you do Aly when you've sold all those tonics, the
wigs and everything, have you thought of that?

He emptied the case of wigs and bottles. Would this be adequate enough? Say he doubled the body up – but how stupid,
it would be far too stiff, no longer flexible. What a fool math-
ematics or anything scientific had never been strong points,
that sort of thing fails you of course throughout life in situations such as this. He sized up the wardrobe, then opened
the doors wide – hopeless, absolutely ridiculous to begin.
He pushed the rug under the bed again, and lay on top – a
waning moon in the middle. How quiet the place seemed
except for the partition that now and then creaked – but
that's just to remind me I'm still alive, that I'm not alone in
all this. He uncurled and went over to the window, thrusting
his flushed face out, welcoming the rain, the coolness. Again
that voice, yes he could swear – but no it's impossible, yet

at the same time? He opened the door, and stood for some time listening – an abyss of time: the epitome of self-pity. At last rewarded, but only by the sound of the front door opening, closing. Back in his room from the window he saw a face upturned, for a moment snatched, then gone. He climbed crab-wise down the stairs. How absurd all this is, of course it wasn't him when – well when – but how can you be sure? You haven't looked in the sober light of day – a case of mistaken identity perhaps, the hour, the place, how can I precisely recall, when the past is an arid landscape filled with a vegetating imagination; that secularisation of the ideal.

Once a letter found in the old man's spidery handwriting, word for word practically learned off by heart:

> I used to have a hundred guilty moments, but I did things just the same, perhaps I liked feeling guilty, it gives one more to think about. I suppose those who indulge in crime like the risk of being found out . . .

The street empty, rain against walls – a dozen cats falling down a well. Berg slowly climbed back, sat for a time on the top stair. Should I write a note to Judith, slip it under the door, arrange to meet her? Why can't she participate in my life now? But would she be desirable still, when there's no sense of betrayal behind my touch, and she more than willing – there would be no risk either way, what possible pleasure can I hope to gain from her now – still a note – far better to stay in her place rather than – well rather than sharing a room with a corpse.

> Just like your father Aly, he used to leave little notes on my pillow you know, before he went off on night duty, yes

little notes with kisses, so he couldn't have been as bad as all that could he now? You're very similar in funny little ways, strange how it comes out like that isn't it?

Perhaps after all it would be best to go back, sit quietly, think calmly. Personal data as compared to world situation – why the feeling of division it's surely the same? If I wish to create then I must first annihilate. Can I compel the stars to revolve eternally round myself? Stay in the room until evening and then . . .

He quickly drew the curtains, switched the light on, and knelt by the bed. A plan developed: first he would take the body down into the hall, 'phone for a cab – though that meant money. He searched for his wallet, and realised there wouldn't even be nearly enough for the rail fare, sufficient for a cab to the station, but what then? The risk, of giving his name the other end, Edith's address, it would create suspicion immediately, not so inconspicuous once declared he couldn't pay for a ticket. But I'm only carrying my father to the burial ground he begged me to take him. Well it's a strange way of taking him, in the middle of the night, in such a way, on such a night? But Officer you know what people are like, suspicious with only what they see and feeding off their imaginations. A parasite living on an action I alone dared committing, how can they possibly convict, or even accuse one who's faced reality, not only in myself, but the whole world, that world which had been rejected, denounced, leaving a space they hardly dared interpreting, let alone sentence. Surely I've served imprisonment long enough, this, now, is my birthright, the after-birth is theirs to cope with, along with the rest of the country's cosy mice in their cages of respectability.

He dragged the eiderdown out and taking this off, half unrolled the rug, but without looking down, he began feeling with his hands. Yes there were the lumps of his father's suit, the stiff body underneath. But to make sure, best to look, take the suit off, see the tattoo marks, then there could be no doubt. He locked the door, and faced the half unrolled rug. No, far better to get away quickly now and find some quiet spot. He made a more compact bundle, gently lifting it up over his shoulders. Strange how light the body was, considering – well considering the old man hadn't been just skin and bones. He could at this rate take along a few belongings. He dumped the body on the bed, and began collecting a few clothes, books, Edith's letters, some bottles of hair tonic, which he put in a carrier bag. The dance hall lights fell on some leaves which threw their shadows against one side of the wall, separating that half of the bed from the body, which in the semi-darkness almost seemed to rise and weave on a dance by itself. Berg took a last look round, before collecting his various bundles, the body over his shoulder. Padding past many closed doors, hardly daring to breathe until he reached the hall, where he dumped everything in a corner, and searched for some coppers. He found three. A light under the landlady's door, could she be asked for the extra penny? Bound to start her usual gossip, no doubt ear to keyhole as soon as he picked the telephone up. What of the others, behind their doors? How could he disturb those he had never actually seen, only heard occasionally the creaking of a bed, a chair, a gasp, the distant humming of radios? He searched every pocket to make sure. Nothing. Perhaps the cafe next door would oblige. The body could be left for a few minutes, it seemed unlikely that anyone would see it in the corner. The street swept up by rain. Scattered about

the road and pavements charred remains of fireworks, bits
of singed, damp rags – relics from another age. Cafe lights
tinselled round the windows, inside red bulbs were hearts
cut out against a perspiring ceiling – a whale's stomach about
to expand, appeared to tremble as Berg entered. Surrounded
by the smell of half-cooked vegetables. Behind the counter a
girl with a twisted safety-pin face served tea or coffee. Berg
bought some cigarettes, pocketed the change, could not bring
himself to ask for any pennies. Nothing for it but to walk to
the station. He marched back into the house, picked case and
carrier bag up, and was about to reach for the body when
he heard someone on the stairs. Judith bearing down. Well,
well if it isn't our sociable neighbour Mr. Alistair Greb, on
the point of departing too I see. In heaven's name there soon
won't be a living soul I know in this place. She stared at the
case, the carrier bag, sniffing, she prowled round Berg, a few
strands of hair trailed over her eyes. Berg manoeuvred into a
position he hoped would hide the body from Judith's inquisi-
tive gaze. He saw the powder on her cheeks had dried into
small particles round her nostrils, and her hair, a blondness
that made one wonder what colour she was elsewhere. An
imitation pearl necklace encircled her flushed neck, a few
of the beads chipped – decaying teeth against three circles
of her neck, above these her scarlet mouth, that yawned
and yawned wider, nearer. Terribly sorry but he had to go,
a telegram you know, mother very ill, though he would
probably be back in a couple of days. She stood always that
much in front, now completely blocking the doorway. He
heard couples laughing as they left the dance hall, followed
by the vibrating, whirring of motor bikes, cars. If he could
only leave right away a lift might be secured to the station.
Judith now in the act of fawning, plucking at his arm, her

fingers already crawling under his frayed cuffs. What a shame Aly, do hope you won't be away long, I mean I shall miss you, you know how it is, I'll miss the light under your door, it's sort of comfy to know someone is near at hand if in trouble, or in need, isn't it? But you'll keep the room on won't you? Maybe you would like me to look after things while you're away? Her eyes lowered, purple lids that gave him an odd erotic sensation, something secretive almost, covering the iris, the pupil, and for a moment he wondered what she might be really thinking, desiring. But then he had no time to question the whims or wiles of any woman. If only she would leave, or at least let him pass. You know of course Nathy's left me, had a dreadful row last night, called me a whore and God knows what – I ask you, me – well good rid-dance I say, a man like that, no respect for a decent woman, and how he drinks – well you saw him, though mind you I must say you weren't so good yourself, I felt quite sick when I saw you both. What did she mean both – when, how, where? Last night of course silly, when you were both reeling here, yes right where we are now. I thought at first you were by yourself, then I saw him, and he started shouting out all those obscenities. I just left you to it, I hate sordid scenes, it's so bad, I mean it looks bad, what people thought I don't know, thank God I was well out of it all. Berg nodded, foot tapping edge of the eiderdown. Squash it completely out of sight. He won't be back this time I know he won't, so here we are Aly and I can wait, you won't be away long, I mean she's not very ill is she, your old Mother? Judith giggled a little, made to elbow Berg as he picked the case up. Well I can see you're in a hurry, so I won't keep you. Don't forget what I said Aly will you, and 'phone me as soon as you're back, from the station? Nodding more vigorously, clutching case and carrier bag he edged towards the door. The body would have to be left while Judith remained in the hall, but as soon as the coast was clear then he could come back and collect it. Right now it was important to evade Judith, so far so good, it seemed she hadn't noticed anything wrong.

Aly what's that dripping from the bag, oh dear look out the carrier bag's breaking. The bag split, bottles of hair tonic rolled across the hall, a few broke, the liquid trickled towards the stairs, divided, ran in tiny streams into the corner. Judith down beside him. Together they began picking up bits of glass, sliding in the tonic that spread in its mucus-like way right round them, between them, over them. A door opened, the light shot across. Berg shrank back, bringing Judith with him, she taking the opportunity of pressing closer; sticky, the tonic now drying – gum from a tree – almost making it impossible for Berg to tear himself away. He felt Judith's warmth, her soft wet tongue in his ear, soon she became intent on biting all available flesh between hairline and collar. But the landlady's demanding voice made her stop. Berg sank back, while Judith squirmed above him. But as soon as the landlady seemed satisfied that no one was about and closed the door, Judith began licking his fingers. He pulled sharply away, until he lay flat on the floor, his head resting against something quite soft. Judith began wiping his clothes down with a large handkerchief that distinctly smelt of wet fur and hard-boiled sweets. He tried getting up, but she leaned over him, and in the half light he saw her lips curl almost – yes almost – he could swear in a sneer, a positive leer, or was he mistaken and it was only the lustful gaze of a frustrated woman? He jerked sideways. Judith fell right across the body. He faced the door, not daring to look round. Soon he heard her hushed voice, that child's tone, intimidated, yet trustful, that twisted something deep inside him. He swayed back, hearing the couples outside shouting, then dwindle away, like stage effects, someone in the props corner had silenced them, now only the rain echoed in the half-empty auditorium. What's in it Aly, it feels like a body, it isn't, I mean you haven't – Aly what's under that ghastly eiderdown? You wouldn't understand, I had to do it, something, no one, especially a woman like yourself would never understand. His tongue an icicle, it would never really thaw for anyone, let alone Judith. He felt her hand pass under his arm, a starfish gliding silently, slowly, knowingly. Aly you don't have to tell me I can guess, it's him isn't it, but I can't look, it is him isn't it rolled up in there, oh Aly love I understand. He bit the inside of his mouth; laughter, absolute deep belly laughter mounted up, now like trying to control a climax. He flung his hands out towards the door, but Judith caught his arm and hung on, murmuring with almost sensual pleasure.

Aware of her mouth creasing into flushed cheeks; the squeaking of cupboard doors, drawers, as Judith trotted about, packing clothes, throwing things haphazardly into cases. Of course she hardly realises the implications, and the fact is she would never admit even to herself that there's such a thing as a dead man in her room, on her bed, that she's about to run off with a murderer. To her it's all a myth. How adaptable women are – practical? No, just irrational to suit their needs, that paradoxical fascination for their anarchy of destruction, yet retaining an air of complete innocence. He almost relished in being with Judith in such a situation, swept along in the attitude she had adopted, more than by his own sense of justification in what he had done. Yet if he unrolled the rug – but crouching right on top – a dog guarding its mistress's treasure: Judith's hat.

I won't be long now Aly, why on earth you didn't tell me in the first place, I can't understand, I mean how you really felt about us, about me. Though I should have guessed all along. Berg trailed two fingers through the dust along the window ledge, while Judith continued patting down some blouses, pulling out cardigans, banging cupboard doors. Of course I knew there was something between us right from the start, that wicked look you used to give me on the stairs, but I must say this, you were always so subtle, the way you used to brush by, touching me so gently just here, yes right here with your elbow, of course you did, no use denying that now. And you know something it always gave me that funny feeling, I mean when Nathy and I used to pass you then get back here well we'd go straight to bed and I'd think of you, wondering what you would be like. Have you had many women Aly? Oh I just wondered, it's one of those things you know that's interesting, not that I go in for statistics in the way of counting one's lovers. Oh Lor' I'm sorry, have I hurt you Aly? Aly there now, what is it? You are a funny chap. Oh dear I nearly trod on it, I mean him. Of course he's very possessive, I mean was possessive, I couldn't even look one-eyed at another man and he'd threaten to slit the poor chap's throat.

Berg opened the window. The rain had stopped, an orange haze lifted the stark trees and roofs out of their usual greyness. He felt Judith's arms encircle him, rubbing his chest, up and down. He rested his head against her, felt her intake of breath. Such acceptance, complete lack of conscience, the sudden transfer of affections, without apparently having their emotional side-effects! Here amongst such softness could there be a centre of real hardness, a steel badge of indifference? As if in her I find a beginning of my own sense of betrayal. That's only because he's not round the next corner, or outside the door, or mounting stairs, the knife ready to slit my throat. Of course that's it, no flesh and blood confrontation, merely a ghost mocking at every sigh, every little delight taken in touch, the smallest gesture, the frenzy, the despair caused by the endless demands of those on the other side. Oh Aly not now, not again, you're a maniac, worse than he was really you are, stop it, oh don't . . . He noticed a slight look of fear, or was it a tinge of contrariness in the blueish fleck of her eyes? Not now sweetie, we better clear out don't you think? She looked at the bed, frowning, biting her lower lip. What shall we do with it? That was relatively simple, a cab could be called, they would stay the night in the next town, didn't she have plenty of money, enough for them to go away, perhaps even abroad – the States, Tokyo, anywhere she wished, start a new life together? She nodded, sighing, as she drew the curtains, then turning from the dust – insects flying out – that collected and drifted up to the ceiling.

Berg sat on the bed, knees sliding together, tracing concentric circles in the eiderdown. Perhaps it wasn't very wise to take Judith with him. Look she must understand something, wouldn't she rather stay behind until he had got rid of it, then he'd come back and collect her? Judith spun quickly round, as though on an apex consisting entirely of her own flesh. How dare you suggest that, you'll be discovered, do you realise that, do you know what you've really done Aly? Murder, yes murder. Whispered as if her tongue and lips had suddenly found perverse pleasure in encircling a foreign word. Her eyes paled, her mouth a slit, which might not widen again. Berg sank back, so that his head rested on the body. Stay here with the bones, linked, him unaware, ocelli merging on the skin. Really Aly I don't understand you, what is it you want, your own suicide, and bring me into the pact, is that what you want? Well I'm damned if I'm staying, and if you have any sense you would clear out too, leave that where it is, not touch it again. Her fingers over his head, twisting round his neck. Aly did you hear me? Nails that were sequins stuck on rubber gloves. Hands wrapping him up, hands fumbling in Christmas stockings, in the back of cars, in the cinema, hands in lavatories, hands round black shiny balls in the tube, and those hands that comforted in the night pliable, flexible cool hands soothing nightmares away. Very well they would go together, but on one condition, the body went with them. Take that, a corpse with us? Oh Aly I've heard of kinky things, but this beats all. What do you propose doing, we'll have it between us in bed I suppose? No, only a short journey in mind then after that, well they could do whatever she wished, go anywhere, wherever she chose. Alone, just the two of us Aly? She fondled the skin between his wrist and cuff. You've got more hair there than he ever had you know. He looked down wondering vaguely about the measured strokes of her hands, noticed his zip unfastened, and underneath? No, no, safely tucked in, but bursting – though surely only a thought, that instrument of pleasure belonged to someone else now.

He tied the eiderdown up with Judith's dressing gown cord, and tested the bundle for weight once more. Lighter than ever, or had he just got used to carrying a body? Really it would be better if he went alone, after all he didn't wish to complicate matters, or in any way compromise her. He would be back as soon as possible, then they could leave together. He went on tying a few more knots in the cord. Judith peered at herself in a compact mirror, applying more mascara. Imagine mornings of that, the curlers, the daily, nightly rituals, that narrow life rounded with domestic walls. He pressed down on the body. But Aly I shall only worry about you, I couldn't bear waiting up here by myself, wondering if they've caught you. It's quite hopeless that plan, now no more do you hear, it's definitely settled, I'm coming with you, and don't let's have an issue about it. She applied a double load of scarlet to her lips. Berg stared at the pattern in the eiderdown, held by a triangle within a circle. Judith wriggled into her coat, chin buried by the ruffle of the fur collar, ready for beheading, and how she smiled, a crack in icing sugar, a little wider perhaps the whole surround would crumble? Well what are we waiting for? I'm ready, or are you staying until the body rises up and walks?

Berg picked the eiderdown up, swaying slightly. You better take two of those cases, I'll manage the rest. I don't know what you're going to do with that Aly, best to dump it on the beach, then we can clear out of town. Berg followed her down the stairs, the cases bumped against his legs, the body slid down his back. Stopping he hoisted it up again. Half way down they saw the landlady emerge and wind up the hall clock. Judith hissed, drawing back. Only when they were sure the coast was clear did they dare to go on, but now like thieves, suspicious even of their own shadows.

The rain had completely stopped. The sound of water over tiles, down windows, from the gutters, rushing away, as if loath to stay in one place, gathering, preparing to invade new territory. It was, of course, far too late for a cab, they would have to walk to the station. But Aly you're surely not taking that with us on the train, aren't you getting rid of it now, look I'll stay here, and mind the luggage, while you pop down to the beach, it wouldn't take you a minute to do that now would it?

> Be a good boy Aly and run down to the grocers for me, you can have an extra sixpence at the end of the week.

They were going to the station, all three, if she didn't like it then she knew what she could do, go back and wait for him. He felt the body bounce on his back as he quickened his step. Judith dragged on to his arm, crying out for him to slow down, her heels digging their bird-marked trail, the mascara congealed blood under her eyes. The infinite variety of the feminine temperament! Once the majestic, self-effacing mistress, almost self-sufficient, the assured emancipation, and now a snivelling creature treading on his tail – but what of the master without his slave? Admittedly it would have been better to have left her behind, far safer in the long run. How she clutched on to him, as a snail to its shell, fearing any moment it would be stamped upon. Oh let's go back Aly, let's wait at least until daylight, it's cold now, I'm so tired, and there won't be any trains at this ungodly hour. She continued dragging on his arm, but he went on, seemingly unperturbed. But Judith wasn't going to be so easily defeated, for she swept suddenly by, and spreading out her arms tried barring the way. Berg veered left, but again she stood before him, they sidestepped like a drunken couple waltzing home. He finally gave in, if only because the weight of cases and the body made any attempt in a physical combat impossible, besides it was wasting precious time. There must be, bound to be, a midnight train home – non-stop.

> When will you be back Aly, write and let me know won't you? I can make your favourite puddings, and we'll buy you some nice new shoes for Christmas, do all the things we used to do.

Someone singing nearby made Berg pause, he pushed Judith into a doorway, and flung the cases, plus the body, into a corner. Strange how that tune – a fly's feelers scratched at the memory – where, when? Ah yes, hadn't the brass band played it only the other day? Soon he noticed a shadow – an ink stain – spread across the pavement. Judith huddled further in the corner. Oh God, oh Christ, who is it, what's going to happen, Aly I'm so frightened? Berg peered out, thought he recognised the outline of a familiar figure swaying up the road. But it's impossible, it's just someone vaguely resembling him that's all, for he's here, rolled up, tied up with her dressing gown cord, with at least eight knots, secure in that corner, ready for cremating or throwing to the worms. Oh Aly let's go back now, come on. She clawed his sleeve; snapping at the construction of thought, whittling down the backbone of decision. He picked up the body, and the cases. Aly you do look strange, so pale, are you sickening for something, do let's go back? He heaved the body further up on his back. Perhaps after all she's right – what and be the prisoners of a combined guilt? The conscience only sets in when one is static. Be master of your chosen fate, don't listen to the nonsensical babble of this whore, a bitch-goddess. Look wouldn't she be happier if he went on by himself now, wasn't it safer considering everything for her to go back and wait? Under my dead body, really Aly what do you take me for? A sudden composure that was more frightening than when defeated. She patted her hair into place, and pulled her hat further down, tucking her chin into the fur collar – a cat any minute about to claw his eyes out. Take up the body and run – run ...

Surrounded by one's own breathlessness, heart beats, each a clock, the mainsprings out of order. Soon he heard Judith clicking up behind. In front the sea stretched, and yawned, waves that were garlands of flowers gathered in by spirals of faint light. Tramps uncurled from under the pier, shaking off sand and pebbles from their rags and bits of newspaper. Yellow creviced faces upturned, stared at the strange civilised couple appearing at this hour. Three of them climbed up, shuffled into a circle, two snatched at the eiderdown, until the body rolled from Berg's back, the cord snapped, the eiderdown – a shoal of fish – spread out before them. Judith shrank away as Berg moved forward, and stood over the rug which alone now covered the body. The men's faces a row of rotten apples strung above him, bent and shook closer. One snatched again, another tried to pluck the rug away. Berg sat on it, staring at the sea. Like sores, their faces, scratch the scabs off, secretions flowing on the stigmata I planned for myself alone. Well be thankful at least Judith had fled, now a retreating figure beyond the bandstand. Meanwhile one of the men had crept up on all fours, making clucking noises. Look they needn't think he had anything to give, sorry misters not a bean. They huddled nearer, hands stretched out. Berg fumbled in his pockets, found sixpence half buried by crumbs in the corner of an inside pocket. He threw it out. They watched in silence, while the coin rolled between the railings. They began to snigger. A tarantula hand claimed a corner of the rug. Berg threw half a crown down which rolled to the edge of the pavement, spun, rolled back and lay at his feet. One of the men pounced on it, bit it. The others made signs, and whimpered, or fawned Berg's legs. One had himself undone, a lump began to sprout. No, no not that, you're very much mistaken sir. They're just children, simple, with simple minds, that's all, a little game they want me to join in. He tried standing up but found himself pinned down, something exploded in his ear. Two either side now; one knelt close, making a loud sucking sound; three, four hands explored the gap between, but two only an inch away. He flung some more money down that scattered into broken scales with the spray, silver-flashing against blue. Four acrobatically bent backwards, then toppled over each other, giggling, scratching one another as Berg gathered up the rug and ran towards the park. The gates were closed. He looked round, fortunately the men had apparently lost interest, were squabbling amongst themselves. Berg noticed his white hands, the veins drawn in with an indelible pencil. The body bumped against his back, once a hand flapped over his shoulder, he shoved it in quickly, aware of the rubbery texture of the flesh – ah well the old man had never been a flesh and blood character really.

He reached the top of the hill that overlooked the station – a deserted penal settlement – surrounded by a cluster of Victorian buildings, either side of the road the houses piled on top of each other, in such a confused order that only bored children might leave their toys in. A startled rabbit ran out from a clump of bushes nearby, hesitated, and as the sun – a metal disque – threw itself upon a sheet of steel and hit the hill, the creature scampered to the other side.

Fingers too hot even for shielding my eyes; incapable, thoughts impotent, fraud underneath, yet all parts longing to join forces, fight the dragons from the north, from the south. Maybe they are formed already inside and therefore what is the point of conjuring something up only to be defeated by it in the end? How heavy the body felt; throw into a ditch, why bother taking it on the train? He sank down on the verge, closing his eyes. Darkness, only darkness, I seem to have drifted into a chaos that can never be clarified, or even justified. He tugged at some grass, letting the pellets of earth fall through his fingers. But I'm not giving in, not now, having come so far, the rest should be comparatively easy. He clutched the top half of the rug, was the head underneath? A slightly oblong shape it seemed, had it been kicked, but dare I look? He continued clasping the rug, almost tenderly, as though it were a treasured possession, and then buried his head in the middle of the folds.

Two white-foaming horses with female heads and hooves of fire, with strands of golden mane – honey cones – bore him across a silken screen of sky, over many islands that floated away, and became clouds, a landscape of snow stretching below, and above a canopy of gold. But a harsh voice needled him, pin-pricked his heart, and three drops of blood poured out, extended across the canopy. From this whirlpool a shape formed, then a massive head appeared, without eyes. He turned to the horses, but they were now toads, squat and squeaking, leaping into the hissing pool. The face grew, the mouth opened, swallowing everything, nearer and nearer, until he felt himself being sucked in, down, down and yet farther down, into quicksands of fire and blood, only the dark mass left, as though the very centre of the earth had been reached. The sun exploded between his eyes. He stood up, practically hurling the rug over his shoulder, and jogged towards the station. An attempt to dismiss the tugging between heart and throat. Fallen into ways where no one in a conscious state would dare to tread; gone astray on a slender thread. There must be some clue, hasn't there been a recognition, a little subjugation from all this? He looked at his boots, at the soles which licked the wet grass. Hearing a train in the distance he quickened his pace. Head on fire, wine over-flowing a thin glass, and if the glass should break? Then the blood could flow on for others to wallow in. But this is a purely personal enterprise, a private concern, why should the spectators be allowed to step in before the curtain finally falls? A sudden recollection of Judith as he caught sight of a woman in a fur coat stepping out of the station, and as if only now, by being reminded of her, did her presence have any effect, and for a moment he cherished the memory of the impact of her body, her round soft belly, the quick relief of her opening thighs, the smell between, like hyacinths, the blue ones that grew in abundance under the garden wall at home. Does memory alone dwell on detail – the fragrance of nostalgia – the way her fingers played at the side of a chair, on a table; the tilt of her head, the lowering of eyes, the false lashes, and their faint smudge on her flushed cheeks. Remember a bird upon snow, dry feathers, as though pressed together by glue; twice you had walked by, unable to look, yet not going on, then touching with your foot, watching the insects crawl in circles, green, bright-eyed.

The station master squatted by a blazing fire. Berg lurked between the barrier and the ticket office. The body he dumped in a corner of an almost empty waiting room. His hands were squashed pork-pies deep in his pockets. Cleaners rattling buckets and brooms, trooped by. A guard stood near the rug, rolling a cigarette, slowly, deliberately, taking immense pleasure in licking the thin paper. Berg hovered between the waiting room and the platform, pressing machine buttons; be buried under mountains of chocolate, cartons of milk, or stretched for all time on chewing gum. The guard pulling out his watch walked away. Berg rubbed his hands while approaching the rug. Didn't it move then? He looked out of the window, the platform empty, the whole station deserted it seemed. He saw the reflection of his ashen face through the thick dust – animal fur – that softened the harsh contours. He fingered his jaw, good God like asphalt, no wonder everyone stared, a positive Bum! Perhaps on the strength of his appearance alone, seen lurking with strange bundles at the station, he would arouse enough suspicion for the station master, or guard, to call in the police. Wiser to have been accompanied by Judith after all, helped to allay suspicions. But how could he have coped with those beady eyes rolling over him, hundreds and hundreds of small round beads with no hope of being restrung? Pushing the rug further into the corner he approached the booking office. A ferret-faced official sniffed out. No trains to Easthaye until four o'clock. Berg turned impatiently away, yet wasn't there that slight relief? He wondered why, then realised that it meant at least half a day's reprieve, in which to think seriously again, decide one way or the other: whether or not to go back and collect Judith.

You never bring a nice girl home Aly, why don't you invite Doris for tea one Sunday, she's a nice girl?

Yes nice to have twice a week against the cinema wall, after a lush film. That was a thought indeed, what would Edith think of Judith, and especially if she found out that – God never, never would she know that, as far as Edith was concerned she would remain Nathaniel Berg's one and only love.

He was the only one I've ever loved – the first I'd slept with and he respected me for it too – well you don't get virgins nowadays.

Let her remain with that image, he would be the last to destroy her idealistic dreams. After all, admit it, haven't I always considered myself an uncompromising idealist? I decided to change my character, therefore shouldn't I be acting the new role? First and foremost: the body must be taken care of, perhaps deposited in the luggage place, then I can go back have a quick shave, clean up generally, produce this new hero to Judith. What's this cor it's mighty heavy, how long do you want it here then? What's rolled up in it eh – a body? Here give us a hand with it mate. Berg stepped back, holding the pink ticket between two fingers, and without daring to look where they had put the rug and its contents, he marched quickly out of the station. He slid between the walls of houses and shops. Strange how he didn't feel quite himself now, as though the body had been an extra limb helping him on his way. He started whistling, but the wind whisked the tune up, so he stayed silent, while tramping through the leaves – chestnuts that cracked – beneath the branches that splayed into fishbones.

Paper-chase games, stones and crossed twigs on the heath; Edith calling, forever calling, a crow to its young. You returning at twilight, footsore, mud-spattered. Sitting later by the fire, curiosity increasing, autumns of inquisitions:

I keep saying Aly you were found sprouting from a cabbage leaf, yes that's it, a big cabbage like the ones Granpy grows up at Westhaye.

A fluffy yellow caterpillar, uncurling, quivering, that strived always for air, yet remained in the undergrowth. Then later, much later, Edith out shopping you looked in her cupboards, discovering the bundle of letters in a pink box:

My darling Edie,

I've been thinking of buying some land on the moon, and thereby staking my claim, and go up in the second or third rocket – would you come with me? There would be no tax to pay up there, and we could build our own little house at the cost of our own labour, and we won't need a roof, no water rates or property tax, imagine that Edie, girlie? I could take our little budgie, and she could do the cooking, as well as the washing up, and fly to earth every week to bring the milk back – then maybe I would take an extra woman from the sun and cast down her offspring to fight the enemy with a death ray extracted from a lunar worm . . .

About the only nonsensical yet coherent letter the old man had ever written, the rest full of jerky sentences, written in the cramped spidery writing, about money, endless jobs.

But Edie love we'll survive won't we, because you know we have each other and our great love . . .

Could she sell her coat, pawn her rings, he had someone very interested in Persian carpets, and there's that one near Grandma's bed, now she's gone – the radiogram that still had another eighteen months to pay off. Her sewing machine.

Well he's never had my sewing machine Aly, I would never part with that, never, even if he hadn't a penny to his name.

Gran's jewellery disappearing; she's too old to notice or care anyway. Coughing, gasping in the downstairs room, eyes that had already seen death. When she's gone we'll at least have an extra bed. And Aunt Flo, night and day, in black velvet, spied on through the keyhole, combing her long white hair, gnarled fingers with their huge rings, like extra knuckles, dipping into trunkfuls of letters and photographs:

Yes there's your father Aly, a fine man isn't he, and he was a handsome boy too, and such a beautiful baby. There look at this one, that's him in the front. There's me – the one wearing the hat with roses all round. In those days we had buses with horses. There was the driver I'd always sit beside and he'd say 'Oh marry me Flo, marry me!'

Sailor-suited, hoop-in-hand; on a donkey, on a swing; on the beach; spilling lentil soup down the brown velvet suit; in Granpy's arms; at Grandma's feet. At nineteen surrounded by three plump girl cousins, their eyes on the sleek, smiling youth who stared into the distance, one hand resting lightly on the silver-knobbed cane, placed at the suitable angle.

Yes a fine clean-living young man your father, all the girls round about adored him. Your mother was a lucky woman really. Of course she appreciates the fact now he's left her. But don't worry he'll be back, he's not the type to harm anyone, he wouldn't even hurt a fly. When he was only this high he'd bring injured birds back, and look after them until they could fly again. He'll be back, and he'll look at you Aly and say 'my what a fine lad you've grown into'. So eat all that dinner up there's a good boy, and grow into a fine man your father would be proud of . . .

The finger that came out, pecked off your pride; the voice that shrieked for nights, then no more in the downstairs room, and only the four-poster creaking, the asthmatic gasps of Aunt Flo, turning over.

Terrible step-father we had, he'd beat us all over, then threaten to again if we told Mother. He'd get so drunk the doctor would be called in to put the leeches on him to suck the mad blood away . . .

As Berg climbed the stairs, the smell of hair tonic wafted after him. He smelt his fingers, and rubbed them against his jacket. Reaching his room he drew the curtains, shutting out the branches that were a mass of charred limbs set against the sombre mid-day light. But it's here inside the images smoulder; another time I would see those very branches splashed with gold, and myself a white-robed figure kneeling by a river that moves over on its side. He slowly washed and shaved, the razor slipped several times, and blood began to trickle on to the clean starched shirt. He changed into another one, and put on his best pin-striped trousers.

> You have to have a presence first of all old chap, sell yourself you know; get a gimmick, then your hair-oil, or whatever, will go just like that, it's not the material but the manner in which the article's sold that counts.

But how to sell yourself, your plans, ideas, dreams to your late father's mistress? Ah they hadn't thought of that, no book, no glossary, no sales talk could ever tell you the answer to that one. He polished his shoes until his reflection could practically be seen. Then pulling the mirror off its rusty chain from above the mantelpiece, and propping it against the bed, he stood back, surveying himself, sideways, forwards, back again. Of course the trousers were a little on the tight side – but it wasn't as if he didn't have a good pair of legs. He smiled but noticed with slight nausea how yellow his teeth were – the bristles of the toothbrush were worn – well remember not to smile, at least not until reaching home – home? Ah how surprised Edith would be, her caressing eyes, so wide, so opalescent!

The four o'clock train must not be missed, still there's plenty of time, and the body? How long did it take before putrefaction set in? If he could only have embalmed it, like the Egyptians used to, but there he had no aromatic oils or spices. Besides did it matter whether or not the body would rot away? Wasn't as if he meant to keep it, after all once on the train – or better still why not let it remain in the luggage place? He stared at his mouth twisting, his whole face seemed to have wrinkled into a dried apricot. Somewhere at the back of his mind, yes he had probably been considering it for some time, but immediately dismissed: such an absurd, fantastic idea: To take his father's corpse back home to Edith – the trophy of his triumphant love for her! In a Greek play they'd have thought nothing of it, considered to have been a duty, the final act of what the gods expected from their chosen hero.

He looked in the mirror again, his face relaxed, admittedly the usual furrows remained on his forehead, under his eyes, from nose to mouth. Straightening his tie, pulling the coat sleeves over his shirt cuffs, he marched out.

He knocked on Judith's door, and waited, threading his fingers. His Adam's apple merged into the knot of the tie. Soon a familiar rustle, and throwing back his head, he puffed his chest out as the door was flung open. Oh it's you, look I've had enough, really don't bother me any more Aly, I'm so tired, so very tired of everything. He saw the glass-domed houses, with their waxen objects, piled on top of one another, and he almost visualised a large notice hanging round Judith's neck PLEASE DO NOT HANDLE. He thrust his hands out as though to embrace her, but she drew back. Well come in for a minute, there's something you ought to see. Handed a letter, a letter with the well-known spider's trail from edge to edge:

Westbourne

My own darling Judy,

Please forgive me, and I know you will, but I just had to leave the other morning, possessed with intense jealousy caused by that good for nothing Greb next door. You see I knew you were interested in him, and I knew he would take advantage of you Judy, and I'm also aware of your weakness. But I've decided to forgive you, because I realise you are of course basically innocent, having a good heart. My own girlie I think only of you now, and long to hold you in my arms, whisper all the things you like to hear, feel you near me once again.

I will be coming back soon, but you must promise me one thing, never invite that chap round again, nor speak to him, even on the stairs, you must swear that Judy – or else. But I know you're not entirely to blame. But there no more, I have forgiven my Judy and that's all that matters.

I shall be holding you soon my love. But before closing there is one small thing my own darling, could you please forward a little money, about ten pounds c/o the G.P.O. of above town: you see I have somewhat run into debt with someone here, and also I haven't enough for the fare to come back. See you very soon my own girlie.

Your own,

Nathy

Berg read the letter twice, noting from where it had been sent, that it was undated. He asked for the envelope. Judith, curled up on the couch, waved towards the wastepaper basket. An indecipherable post mark. So you better clear out while the going's good Aly, that is if you want to keep your skin. She leaned over, plucking a cushion's tassels; bracelets jangled, flashed, her upper lip slightly lifted. Berg looked at the letter, turned it over, as though hoping to find some clue the other side. Apart from the fact the old man had left the other morning, it could have been written any time, the space between the party and the actual murder say? You fool how could he have ever travelled to Westbourne and back in that time – ah what more proof do I need? By the way I hope you've got rid of you know what, or you are in for real trouble Mr. Greb. She obviously doesn't care a damn now, not one bit, the old whore, the bitch. He stalked past, opened the door, heard her laughing, the bracelets clash behind him. Just a minute before you disappear for good I want my dressing gown cord back, after all that could be quite incriminating for me. He turned threw back his head; now it's my turn to laugh. Instead a dry sort of croaking noise escaped as he stepped backwards.

He pressed against the banisters, in the distance a clock struck four. In his room he undressed, and lay naked, shivering, on the bed, listening to the rain falling through a hole in the ceiling, where the stain had spread and darkened one side of the wall.

Fingers scratching the partition. Two beasts emerging, some-where between head and belly; substantial food for only one, the third lingering, then leaps and devours everything, the remaining two face each other, which will die, the one above, or the one below? There I've lost interest in being the ring master, but shall I remain the impassive observer? Berg pressed himself against the partition, until it shuddered, and he thought someone coughed the other side, a rasping sound that – why yes unmistakeable – and yet?

> Your father never did have a good constitution, but then I knew how to look after him, he used to always say 'Edie love I swear you'd nurse me back from the dead if you had the chance'. He'd even go green, yes all over, at the mere sight of a spider, dear knows where his blood went to then!

Blood, oh yes there had been blood, remember it oozing out of the old man's neck – the old man's? My God whose then, and was it safe at the station, maybe by now they were about to trace the ticket, a matter of hours, minutes, with the light of day? There could be no further delay, he must go back, collect the body, leave by train, any train. Buildings gathered in by darkness; bill boards stark against a purple sky. This time I have to go through with it, look right inside, look at the face, those eyes. Of course Judith might have fixed up that letter, anything for a lark, or rather for revenge, how was he to know she wasn't actually luring him into some trap, already in league with the police? He looked round, almost expecting to see someone shadowing him. The street, a ringless finger, curved past the closed doors, the curtained windows. Safe enough, at least for the moment. The leaves were sun-baked lizards stirring towards the sea that churned its chain of silver snakes, which would, if given half the chance, coil round, pull him out of this urban setting, vomit him on dry land. The station closed. Could he invade the place? After making a careful detour, he decided to climb on to the luggage office roof. He heaved himself up, one or two slates cracked under his weight; he crouched, waiting, until he felt sure no one had heard. Slowly, cat-padding towards the skylight, which he levered open with his pocket knife, and lowered himself down. Striking a match, he looked round, several mice startled by the light were transfixed for a moment, then regaining their senses darted round behind the luggage racks. He searched for his ticket, but failed to find it. He heaved some of the cases off the shelves. Perhaps the body had already been discovered – been smelt? Judith might have informed them that he was station-bound? He threw package after package, case after case down, soon he was so surrounded that he found it difficult to clamber out in order to reach a corner of a shelf where – yes – there it was, the rug at last, and inside? But thinking he heard someone approaching he quickly picked up the rug and standing on a chair pushed it through the skylight, hauling himself after it. Later there would be time to look, in a more discreet place, then perhaps then the mystery could be solved. He clasped the rug, as he might a child, and cautiously stepped across the roof. At the edge he realised the body would have to be thrown over, the thought almost paralysed him; supposing something broke, an arm, a leg? The very idea of carting a mangled corpse around seemed a nightmare to say the least. However there seemed no alternative but to let go. He raised the rug – how light it was, as if yes as if there's nothing inside. He threw it down, soon hearing the dull thud below. Gripping the tiles he pressed down, momentarily seeing his shadow on the opposite wall, a falcon about to hurl itself upon its prey. Through space, suspended almost, then the shock of meeting the ground. Let it just be like this for an eternity, like before waking up properly, or could it be before birth, half in, half out? They said my head was in the wrong position. She must have conceived on her side. Perhaps I liked it that way, maybe that's the cause of my never really finishing anything? Maybe women felt like this after being made love to? What could it be like having heavy pendulous pears strung practically round one's neck, a triangular fur piece, blood every lunar month? Edith? A part of her, he would never know, a consciousness undeclared, a bride hardly virginal that vamped your dreams, a cry in the dark, clutching bouquets through the night's half orgies, a hand groping for the light switch, staring into the mirror after midnight, the hangman's steady gaze at the empty bed, the familiar furniture and objects scattered about the room, yet no longer belonging. The noises behind walls, the faint tapping – convicts sending out signals to the distressed. Murder they whispered to your heart's ease, and you shouting for attention. Edith entering, her eyes half-closed, listening to a sphinx's secret, hiding under the pyramidal palaces of her flesh, no answer to your insistence. And Judith? Is it really too late? If only circumstances had been different – no, not that you fool – even if you had met her given the perfect circumstances, she would never have looked at you. She's obviously the type who prefers maturity, however warped. Besides she's not the sort he would normally look at twice. Then how come this perpetual desire, that creeps and seizes a hold? A desire to know everything about her, the colour of her hair before touching it up, the way she might sit up suddenly, or slowly stretch out in bed, in the mornings the curve of her back, her dream murmurs. Is it all too hopelessly late to know such intimacies? Surely an idle dream, where the point of reality? Conjured up in the imagination anyway, not as if she's the only woman in the world, there are others, more enticing, more willing, even if it meant paying for their charms. Judith a bitch-goddess, no doubt about it, the old man should have cleared out ages ago. But hadn't he returned? And in the rug, what exactly is wrapped up in there? He crawled towards the dark bundle, that had half unrolled, carefully he pulled a corner of the rug. Absolutely nothing there, not even blood stains, nothing at all to give a clue, or remind. Suddenly as if everything was too much to cope with he slumped forward, burying his face in the rug, his arms covering his head so that he no longer heard the sea hissing.

The sun a searchlight hovered over him until he opened his eyes. How long had he slept? Looking round he noticed a crowd had gathered outside the station. He recognised two of the tramps standing quite near, who sniggered as he turned away. He stood up, and only then realised that the rug lay open before him, for a long time he stared at it. Oh God what had happened to the body? They probably all know, those bloody bastard-bums playing their dirty tricks again. He faced them, but out of the corner of his eye he noticed a guard by the station gates. He rolled the rug up and stepped awkwardly across the road, aware of the crowd now bursting into high-pitched giggles, fortunately the piercing whistle of a train drowned them.

Perhaps all has been a dream – the climbing over the roof and everything. Looking back, he wondered how in fact he had managed scaling such a high wall, or even jumped from such a height. When the beginning, where the end? How the sun poked the corners of his eyes. Not a dream at all, a conspiracy they had worked up against him, they had dared putting their fingers in the spoke of the machine he alone had set in motion. But it must go on revolving its full circle, if stopped in any way it would cripple him – let it go on spinning, away from the conditioned milieu, into space, the wild ecstasy of free far-flung moments, catching glimpses of an eternity.

He walked down to the Front, and leaned over the faded-blue railings, staring at some children digging up worms. He leaned further over, Judith approached from under the pier. Good now there's no time to lose, didn't he still have the key to their room, he could make a thorough search and perhaps solve everything.

Half way across the park he slowed down, two men were busy shovelling earth from the path on to a flowerbed. Hadn't that been the very spot where his father had buried the blasted budgerigar? He approached slowly. The men leaned on their shovels, shook off their caps, and wiped their foreheads. One jerked his head at the ground. Some kids, or a raving lunatic mucked this nice bit up, would you credit it, some pays their taxes for places like this, and others go all out mucking it up, not fit for law-abiding citizens is it? Berg nodded. Had they found anything? Why what do you expect mister, a body perhaps? They laughed as he turned his back, and he heard the scraping of their shovels until he reached the gates. It could have easily been another flowerbed, or some dog had scraped the earth back, eaten the bird, hardly now a matter worth pursuing further, there were far more important things to settle.

The curtains drawn in their room. A distinct confectionery smell, a staleness that stifled. He opened the dressing-table drawers, the wardrobe – but what am I hoping to find, an unidentifiable body? He caught sight of his reflection: Machiavellian to say the least, rather startling to see the surface revealing in fact so much of what he only partially felt. How macerated the cheeks were, fairly sunken in, making his eyes so huge, his neck mottled, stork-like. He sat on the bed. The situation had somehow assumed exaggerated proportions. Before long he would be ill with worry, if not already. Perhaps best to leave, right away, clear out of the place, the town altogether, forget about the whole thing. But could he, now, with a corpse missing, afford the risk of leaving, and still there's the question of money. Very well he'd remain and write to Edith, persuade her to send a cheque, perhaps by then, in a few weeks' time say, when things had settled down a little, he could move on. He looked round the room, at Judith's clothes on the chairs, the bed, the floor, the taxidermal objects piled in the corner – had they been the old man's then? Something he hadn't thought his father capable of having a fancy for – or more rightly a fetish, there were so many! He suddenly noticed a small yellow object on the table, like one of those tattered powder puffs women produced from their bulging handbags. He picked it up. No mistaking this, the same, the only one, the blasted bird, with its brown slits for eyes. Who had unearthed it then, was this the very clue he had been hoping for? He put it down, fingering the dry feathers, feeling the earth peel off, as he left the room.

In his own domain he switched the radio on and listened to the crackling, the whistles that preceded the required station. If a body had been discovered it might be reported – but a body every hour, so they say? In that case they would hardly waste time reporting on one discovered in a minor seaside resort, out of season too. Someone coming up the stairs made him switch the radio off. He pressed against the wall, heard their door open, then close. It was obvious he couldn't remain here forever, even for a couple of days without Judith, or someone, noticing the slightest movement, a step across the floor, the light under the door, she would soon grow suspicious, maybe already she practised the art of listening the other side of the partition?

As he stared at the wigs, that still lay scattered about the room, a brilliant plan, like a butterfly settling on a large flower in a huge but otherwise bare garden, grew into formation. That's it, the very thing, why hadn't he thought of it before, though at the beginning a question of real non-identity had not been such a problem. Disguised as a woman he could move about completely unharassed, as long as the landlady didn't see him; Judith would come to the conclusion that a new lodger had arrived, and if the old man had returned, well then neither would be bothered very much about who lived next door, only thankful that good for nothing bum Greb had at last left. The question of clothes could easily be solved, once Judith went out again, it would take only a couple of minutes to pop into their room, take some things, which she had obviously discarded at the back of the wardrobe, and there he'd be, fully equipped to act how he pleased. The plot is undoubtedly thickening, but the prospect of a further masquerade excited him, and he waited impatiently for Judith to leave.

Not until evening did he hear her clicking down the stairs. He waited until she disappeared round the corner of the street, before entering their room. Soon he found a skirt, jumper, stockings, and a pair of shoes. Solemnly he tried them on, and hobbled across the room, gesturing, fluttering his hands, as he had seen Judith so often do. Quickly he went back to his own room and put the whole disguise on; the nylons against his legs gave him an almost erotic pleasure, but once he had everything on, he felt somewhat hampered by the unfamiliarity of such apparel. Putting one of his best auburn wigs on, he patted it into place, and arranged the fringe until it came well over his forehead and met his eyebrows. What about makeup? He went back to their room.

He handled the cosmetics tentatively, then slowly powdered his face, his hands shook so much that at first he made a mess with the mascara – what a ritual, all to flatter the ego of man – the vanity of woman! He peered into the mirror and nearly toppled over the dressing table with laughter; if only the navy were in, and for a moment he mused on the possibilities, the delights of the adventures he could have had in such a disguise. So taken up with his new appearance that he did not notice the door opening, and only when he heard a familiar coughing and gasping did he look up and see reflected in the mirror, behind his clown-like face, swaying towards him the old man, clutching a bottle of scotch, wheezing, smiling, slobbering. Judy girlie, my little woman, my lovey, look your old lover's back, aren't you pleased to see me? Berg stood up and faced the tottering figure, the outstretched hands. Judy sweetie, what's the matter, aren't you pleased I'm back eh? Oh I know I'm a little sloshed, but hell you can't blame a chap for a drop now can you? Judy it's been a long time, Christ it has, I want you girlie, come on now, let's make up for lost time shall we, you want it don't you, I know you, of course you do. Why what's the matter love, don't be standoffish now with your old Nathy?

Berg felt his arms caught, the bare flesh between elbow and the sleeve of the jumper caught between finger and thumb, and though his father reeled with drink he seemed possessed with an almost demonic strength as he began pulling him towards the bed, whereupon reaching it, he pushed Berg on to it so hard that he bounced several times in the middle. Ah that's it, all the fun of the fair, sweetie take your things off, I want you, I want you Judy do you hear? and I'll make you scream like you sometimes used to, oh sweetie I've missed you, it's been a long time hasn't it? And that chap's gone I think, I hope you haven't been with him Judy while I've been away eh, you haven't been misbehaving have you? My love come here, take those things off, here let me help you, I'm not all that sloshed you know. Fingers running up his legs, further and yet further up. This is how it had been, with Edith, with Judith, how they must have revelled in it, giggling, panting, helping the old man's hands, opening their thighs, unsnapping their suspenders, arching their backs, opening up everything, wide – wider. Lead him on, lead him right there, produce it in his face, in his ear, in his eye, let him have it, so he'll remember to the day he dies. A flowerless stalk waving in the wind – a frog leaping – and in one bound there over the old man's stained waistcoat, now away. Looking down Berg saw his father roll over the bed, the whites of his eyes, legs in the air, then sideways, on to the floor, now motionless. Quick, feel his pulse, but of course that's too much to hope for, strong as an ox, even now he seemed to be moving slightly, moaning a little, his eyes flickering, though his face strangely grey. Berg lifted him back on to the bed, then put a flannel under the cold water tap, and there above his made-up face reflected, which made him remember how the rest must look. He flung the flannel back, it really wouldn't do for his father to be that much revived, best to leave him to figure the scene out – a drunken orgy, a whisky nightmare soon forgotten. He took the high-heels off and ran out. Just in time for he heard Judith returning as he entered his room and bolted the door. Were all plans destined to be so absurdly ambushed?

A point in suffering when pain over-rules everything; I am pain, until it becomes an inanimate object, I look down, wondering when it belonged. Yet each time in its midst it's the worst that's ever happened, nothing goes beyond this, therefore you become optimistic, life is worth living again, perhaps despair's only saving grace, until the next time, and you fall even lower – the abyss eternal! First aware when you were barely ten; clutching a bottle of iodine, stealing behind the bushes at the bottom of the garden, soon came the burning, the screams, but it wasn't – couldn't possibly happen to you: the stomach pump, their faces, endless questionings, counteracted only by the comfort of smooth white hospital walls, the rows of beds. Later the wonder, the miracle of coming back from the dead, of running, leaping with the wind past the river, head over heels once more in the valley, making peace with God, yet secretly making pacts with the devil.

Just lying here for an hour since the sun had filtered through the snow that snail-trailed across the window. How silent the place is, as if the snow had penetrated the walls, sound-proofed the habitual early-morning scurryings, the alarms. Once a huge snow ball, made entirely by yourself, hiding behind the shrubbery, blistered fingers against your mouth, listening for Edith's steps; her Sunday-best hat

knocked off, her flushed face as she took you inside, produced the leather strap, the buckle end for you, for naughty
boys who never love their mother. The white arms with
veins, dimples and wrinkles at the elbow; you static over her
knees, she rhythmically moving, the pleasure in her eyes,
the pleasure that was yours. The sheer delight of not giving
in to a single cry, and afterwards running out, blinking back
the tears, whistling, splashing yourself with water. Later her
sighs, her soft kisses covering the bruises, the wiping away
of blood that took longer, far longer than the cause.

But who cried now? Jerking sobs – a vehicle that might
stop, start up a hill. Berg leaned towards the partition.
Definitely a woman crying, Judith by herself? Impossible, for
such a woman surely an audience is invaluable? He pressed
himself closer, then as the sobbing merged into howls, he
tapped several times on the partition, to be instantly rewarded
by absolute silence from the other side. He tapped again, this
time however a fierce knocking answered him. He quickly
dressed, all previous plans now forgotten. Judith in distress
needing his help, advice, sympathy, obviously alone, what
else could he do? He had more or less been invited in, his
help requested. Though once outside their door he hesitated
before knocking; maybe she had the idea he was someone
else, that indeed a new lodger had arrived! When she saw
who it was he'd be turned away, or she'd grow more hysterical, accuse him of God knows what, disturb the whole house,
cause worse trouble than a few moments of being with her
might be worth.

Besides what would be gained from the situation – hardly
a reversal from the last scene that had occurred?

He knocked, but without waiting for an answer entered.
He's gone, oh God he's gone and taken everything, he'll never

come back now, what shall I do, what can I do? Berg stood in the middle of the room, stroking the velvet-covered couch, occasionally picking off stray bits of cat's fur, and flicking them on to the floor. Best to wait until she's had a good cry, no sense out of her at the moment, hardly aware of my presence, crouched half-naked on the bed, clutching the pillow, biting a corner of the sheet. Gradually the moaning stopped, the sniffs subsided, and her breathless monologue now took on more calculated sentences. Fancy coming back, daring to come here, pretending he was ill, swearing he'd had a stroke, then sneaking out without a word, in the middle of the night, taking my money, my jewellery, and my fur coat, the dirty rotten swine. Well I'm through, I've had enough, I'm going to call the police, he won't get away with it, I'll drag him right down, fancy doing such a thing to a vulnerable woman like myself, taking advantage of me, my sympathy, my love, well he can go to hell and rot there for all I care now, after all these years. I wouldn't mind if he had told me, you know, had it out mutual like, come to an understanding, if there had even been another woman involved, though mind you I'm not sure there isn't knowing him, he can't do without it for long, greedy old hog, he's the sort that will be at it when he reaches a hundred, and God help us if he does. Well what do you want, I thought you had gone for good? He's nothing but a dirty rotten coward, 'cos that's all men are, they can't face up to life, or themselves, no moral responsibility whatsoever. And to think I felt sorry for him, thought he looked a bit sick. Wait until I lay my hands on him, wait until I see him, he won't have a chance, once I call the police in. He owes bills left right and centre, don't I know it, I've had to pay them off, well I suppose I've been a fool. Men make me puke, all they really care about is putting their pricks up anything that's going.

We had arrears in rent – oh months to pay, so I went to the landlord, begged him not to take us to court – even asked if I could work for him – me – fancy me doing a thing like that. He was very nice told me not to worry. But we had to leave of course.

Berg watched Judith's blotched, mottled face rise out from the bedspread, flat between the wall, the partition. Well what do you want, standing there as though you've seen a ghost, haven't you ever seen a woman humiliated before? She gave a shrill laugh and started wiping the corners of her eyes with the sheet. Berg produced an initialled handkerchief, and only after he had handed it over did he realise it bore the initials A. B. He held the handkerchief for her, wiped her cheeks gently, slowly, while she stared up, wide-eyed, almost like a child, and for a moment he caught a glimpse of how she might have been when a girl. Well, well this is a surprise, you certainly know how to dry a woman's tears, maybe you've got a heart after all? He murmured something, pocketed the handkerchief, aware of her half-exposed breasts, the nipples, tiny, deliciously hard. One awkward movement and he could fall on top, bury himself here, there. As if realising, Judith shivered and pulled her cardigan round so that it covered her to the neck. Thank you that's all right, here give it to me. She snatched the handkerchief out again, and rubbed her face until it was shining and red. There that's better. She gave a somewhat wan smile. Berg straightened up, pulling at his tie. He'll probably be back, just a joke perhaps. Some joke, my God, creeping out like that in the dark, stealing my things; he's gone this time, and a good job too, but he won't get away with it, I'll trace him, degrade him until he won't dare to even look himself in the mirror, which he's so bloody fond of doing. Lor' but I'm exhausted, emotionally exhausted Aly. What about a cup of tea love, be a dear and put the kettle on will you, there's a good boy I can see you're well house-trained, I suppose that's Mum's doing? Wish I'd had mine for longer, she died when I was two, never knew my father, didn't even put his name down on the certificate. That's right in the caddy on the third shelf, matches on the second to bottom, all right love? May as well light the fire while you're at it, so freezing, is it snowing? She swept back the curtains, and Berg heard her gasp, exclaim, as he watched the blue flames light up round the stove. How quickly her moods changed with external events, and if he should stay, for other mornings, to light the gas, potter about between the velvet-covered couch, and the table with its knick-knacks, his best pin-striped suit hung outside the wardrobe, his cracked leather boots beside her blue fluffy mules, and watch her wash his shirts and iron them. But supposing the old man returned? Well wasn't that exactly what he had hardly dared to hope for. But then supposing he didn't come back? Stranded here, mornings, afternoons of making tea, playing rummy, attempting to meet the moral obligations Judith presumably expected. No it wasn't worth it. No? Not even for the warmth, the comfort of her arms at night, knowing if he went out, he could come back, someone to welcome him, know at last he belonged to one person who he would be responsible for? No, no, certainly not, she'll only eat you whole, drain everything out of you within a week. Why had the old man left? Precisely because he couldn't stand any more of her, for that very reason wasn't it, hadn't he once said women were more or less consistent parasites?

Kettle's boiling Aly love, don't forget to heat the pot, make it strong, can't bear that dish-water stuff. No, no sweetie, always take the pot to the kettle, that's right, that's my boy. Balancing the tea-pot, the cups, he swayed towards her. Oh do be careful you'll have the lot over, oh dear, there what did I say, oh Aly my best china cups, oh Lor' here let me have the pot. He went down on his hands and knees, picking up the bits, as Judith swept to and fro, mumbling to herself, grumbling at him, at the world. Already he wanted to jump out of the window, and he had barely been with her half an hour. He must get away, now, now before it's too late.

There that's better, do you take sugar, I always forget, one or two? Four! goodness we are sweet-toothed, now he never took it, didn't like anything sweet, cakes or chocolate, nothing like that, though mind you he did have a fancy for savoury things, those cheesy biscuits, and olives, black ones too, can't take them myself, but he really did enjoy them. When we first met, I asked what he liked for breakfast, said he adored olives, imagine that, well of course I didn't believe him, but he swore it was olives he adored, something about it being in the blood, I suppose he thought it classy to say he liked them for breakfast. Dreadful snob, talked of being related to a Marquis, plus an ancestor being an actor, more famous than someone called Garrick I think, yes swore he was descended from this actor of the Middle Ages, there he'd be pacing this very room, flinging his arms out, as if he were on the stage himself. They all seemed a poor rum lot to me, never quite made it, fate he'd say, a family curse. Some other ancestor supposed to have composed Gilbert and Sullivan's music, apparently took all his work to Gilbert, or was it Sullivan, I forget, anyway he never saw it again, until he heard it six months later, by then it was too late to reclaim it, no one believed he had really composed it of course. As if anyone would do a thing like that, but Nathy believed it, persecution mania him and his sort suffer from I think. More tea love?

Berg leaned over, passed his cup to her, leaned further, swaying slightly, as one does at a height, the space below infinitely more compelling – yet the door only a few yards away. She handed him his cup, he sank back. The room closed in, the furniture, walls collided, compressed between it all, any minute, any moment now he'd burst out of the lining. You look a little cold Aly, why don't you sit nearer the fire? Come over here sweetie, there we are isn't that better? Funny he was the same, felt the cold terribly, and oh dear if he hadn't anything in his tummy he'd nearly faint, go all white, yes absolutely white. Two yards away her legs, dark hairs from the ankles upwards. Red toe-nails peeping out. He looked up at her smile of triumphant satisfaction. That same look once with a girl after school, leading you to a point of madness in the playing fields, and afterwards your pretence to the others, who you knew full well she had equally sprung her virgin's vengeance upon. I wonder where he's gone, I don't like to really call in the police, you know what they're like, cynical lot, probably wouldn't believe a word I said, honestly what chance has a woman on her own these days? Now my hubby, bless him, oh no he isn't dead, at least not as far as I know, anyway he would never have treated anyone like Nathy does. Berg continued watching the circles spread in his cup. No Nathy doesn't care a damn about anyone but himself. I blame his parents of course, they, from what I could make out, spoilt him madly, you see they were both frustrated, the father apparently married the wrong sister, you know how it was in those days, went off to India, or somewhere like that, sent a letter of proposal, but as both girls' names began with A, Alice and Amanda I think, he got them muddled, wrote to the wrong one, well so the story goes, he came back, and there she was waiting, the oldest one, Alice, all prepared for the wedding, so he couldn't back out, and I suppose she anyway knew he didn't love her, so when Nathy arrived she turned all her affections on to him. The father went off to India periodically, or somewhere like that, while the mother ran up colossal accounts at all the big stores, and when he came back he had all those bills to face. Then if he didn't bring her presents if he only went for a walk, there'd be an almighty row, she sulking until he had to go and bring something back for her. So Nathy soon learned how to get most things out of life. He blames his parents for setting him off on the wrong foot. His father apparently refused to pay Nathy's training fees to be a singer, 'cos that's what he really wanted to be – imagine him a singer Lor' I don't know what he used to be like but he positively croaks nowadays; anyway to proceed, his father bought him a hat shop, expecting his son to make quite a business out of it, but Nathy spent whatever money he made on taking girls out and having a good time, of course the shop failed, and everything else Nathy took up, until his father tired I suppose of the whole business, died and left Nathy to look after an invalid mother, which of course he didn't, as far as I can gather he met some woman, whom he quickly married, so she could housekeep, and look after his old mum, while he continued gallivanting about – I don't know it's a wonder God allows people like that to go on living, but then it might well be to give them a chance to redeem themselves, but Lor' he never will though strange thing is he's always talking about death, the conscience, God and things like that, I don't understand him – oh dear where do you suppose he's gone? Perhaps he really was ill last night, I should have taken more notice, maybe he's dying this very minute out in a street, frozen to death in the park, yes I know he's taken my fur coat, but he did look quite pale last night, now I come to think about it, and I know he suffers from his stomach, I keep telling him to have an X-ray, I mean he might have an ulcer, and supposing it's burst? Yes, yes perhaps you're right, I ought to sit tight and he'll probably be back before the day's out. Put some more water in the pot love, and switch the radio on, it's the left knob turn to the right.

Mechanically Berg found himself obeying her instructions; aware of the room darkening, and as he came back with the tea-pot, he could hardly see Judith, just a blurred outline, and outside the roofs covered by snow. Of course it's warmer in the house, in this room, than in my own place. But something continually nagged at the back of his mind, something that had to be seen to. As he poured the tea out he remembered – of course, the body! But whose body, where was it now, would it be traced to him? Maybe after all he was in the safest place, one step outside would be fatal. Though it might be worse here with a woman who had actually witnessed him carrying a corpse, who could so easily turn nasty if he happened to say the wrong thing, do something that didn't suit her. Strange she hadn't mentioned anything, though perhaps not so surprising considering how emotionally she was caught up. Always the chance though that she would remember, recall any moment, then where would he be, what could he say, pass it all off as some sort of hoax, swear there had never been a body in the rug at all, purely her imagination? She couldn't have seen very much, just the clothing perhaps, come to that he hadn't either, at least not since the time he had half unrolled the rug, felt the body, but you hadn't looked. In fact the whole scene now appeared a faded negative, something he had begun but not developed. Best to let things slide, take care of themselves. But as he sipped his tea, and Judith continued chattering, as the snow piled up on the window ledge, and moth-like fell upon the buildings opposite, the problem arose from that store house in the mind, where all things unpleasant are wrapped up for a time, until something – a self-imposed injection – perhaps makes it react, or a knock hardly at the time felt, but later confronted by the bruise. Judith, how would she feel, what would she really say if he was discovered, proved guilty, of having murdered someone? Hadn't he at one time desired to be someone in her eyes, taller than the tall, would she accept someone who killed not just for lust's sake? Busy making up her face, pencilling her eyes, eyebrows, so that for a time she remained silent, concentrating on transforming herself, pursing her lips, eyes screwed, nose wrinkled, twisting her head. She would never accept anything or anyone out of an order, however chaotic it might be in the end, she set for herself, and for others who stepped into her circle. Even if he explained, played upon the deception of doing it for her sake, would her conceit allow such a thing? Do turn the fire up love, it's getting colder than ever. There I feel much better now, I must say you've helped me Aly, you are quite understanding really. What about something to eat, there's some eggs and bacon, won't take me a tick?

Berg stared out of the window. The street bound by snow-drifts. He leaned out. Icicles hanging from pipes – splinters of glass – reflecting the shadows from clouds. A muffled town assuming the atmosphere of a cathedral, a sacrilege if one spoke above an ecclesiastical whisper. Sizzling of frying, the warmth of the room, and Judith softly humming, brought a sudden sweep of nostalgia; a tangle of broken wires, a need to gather them up, sort out, graft together, encircle the mind, the body, thus bound, motionless become, and in becoming: know. He banged the window down. Terribly sorry but he couldn't stay for anything to eat, just remembered about an appointment – with the dentist . . . Oh what a pity, look I've fried two eggs for you, some nice crispy bread, do stay won't you Aly? He backed towards the door, smiling, head shaking. His hand sliding over the handle. Do hope things sorted themselves out – so sorry must go. Judith straightened up, wiping her hands on the plastic apron with its large printed roses, smoothed her dress down that met the knees which like swollen suns swivelled round the dimples that were knotted mouths behind their twisted stocking seams. He closed the door before she could say anything more, and for a time he remained on the landing, breathing deeply, as though he had just emerged from a wide but shallow pool.

Crossing the park: a subterranean world surreptitiously risen; here a million star-fish pinned on the forelocks of a hundred unicorns driven by furious witches. A transformation that held itself occasionally in suspense, but for how long would it be like this? Even as Berg made his way the wind shifted the snow between the trees, leaving divisions as in a map. At times the snow came practically up to his knees compelling him to clutch the branches in order to gain higher ground. At one point a light flashed through the semi-darkness, straight into his eyes, then out again, as though a photograph had been taken. He stopped, anticipating its reappearance, maybe only a space between the trees, perhaps even the sun? Another flash then out – fixed, developed for all time, imprinted on newspapers, magazines, condemned, judged, or worse, dismissed THIS WAS THE

MAN READ ALL ABOUT THE STRANGE LIFE OF ONE WHO
NEVER RETURNED.

He walked on, past the many shapes, and forms that rose
and fell, or crawled towards him, pulled his hair, tugged his
clothes, and in the distance the whispering of an orchestra
without a conductor, playing no familiar piece, so it was hard
to tell whether it was the wind, or the distant throbbing of
the sea, as against the more distinct tones of human beings.
Is there still a world outside this area? Of course there is, you
fool, you can't expect to be a god and switch life on and off
like an electric light. No, it's far simpler, you just allow it to
drift on, if lucky enough you drift with it. But I refuse to be
swept out, or even in-shore; I shall remain mid-ocean; then
what are you doing here? Surely it's no more than a matter
of chance, but who sets it off to begin with?

> Throw it Aly, that's right throw the ball to me, straight
> now, oh silly thing, there it's gone over the hedge, run
> and find it, quick now.

Soon he saw parts of the Front emerge, the pier with its
turrets, lights that held the sea in patterns of blue and gold.
The only sound came from some children, screaming as
they hurled snowballs at one another, who spread out as he
came through the gateway. Giggling, pressing the snow into
small hard missiles they waited. He dived through and ran
towards the station. They'll never get me, with their sticks
and stones, never, ever.

> But why do they do it to you Aly, what was it you did, what
> was it you said, it must have been something, they can't
> victimise you without having a cause now can they?

The station a discarded film set as he passed through the barrier. The only sign of life seemed to be in the waiting room, crammed full of destitutes rubbing themselves, each other, or crouching over the fire. Someone began making signs at Berg, then suddenly shifted, fingering buttons, shuffled towards him. He made to turn abruptly away, but he felt the other's hand on his arm, he wrenched himself free, staring angrily back. The man, who had a scar on his left cheek, grinned, pointing at a door marked private. Berg shrugged; the chap's obviously an idiot, if not that then positively perverted. His arm caught hold of again, and this time he was pulled towards the door, led into a yard, where the snow had been swept up into frozen cygnets in the corners. In the middle of the yard a rubbish heap, nearly as high as the surrounding wall. But why had he been pulled in here, a back-yard, was the chap a nutcase? Perhaps he'd find himself strangled, dumped on the rubbish pile. Best to get away now, before it's too late. But even as he made for the door he noticed the man pointing at the rubbish, and there precariously balanced on top – was it – could it possibly be? He edged towards it, slightly aware of the man shuffling close behind, his heavy breathing. He saw an old packing case nearby, which he pulled over to the rubbish heap, climbing on this he reached up half way. Little by little the rubbish fell away, rags, newspaper, old shoes, bottles, tins, until at last he reached the dummy, which he gently pulled down. The case gave way. Berg toppled over.

These things have a way of turning round on one Aly, he'll pay for what he's done, even if it's only his conscience he's left to live with, though mind you I often wondered whether he ever had one.

Through revolving tunnels, sliding doors of white, and a grizzled face bending over you. Somewhere in the distance laughter broke out, no, no, it's someone whispering, and the sound of water gushing, rushing through the pipes, the gurgle down the drain.

> It isn't true Aly is it, you wouldn't do a thing like that, I mean to say you're not one of those, not my boy, not my own son?

The face blurred, himself limp, a stain, a mere stain left, in a station back-yard at a seaside resort. He's gone now, he's finished, buttoning himself up, the door swinging, the sniggering running through a steel track from thorax to thigh.

> I can't understand it myself, how they can, I must admit women give me all the pleasure I want, I mean don't they old chap? I don't believe people when they say oh I've tried everything and the only thing left is to turn queer.

Clutching the dummy, Berg slowly left the yard. The thing to do now, the only thing, would be to catch an express train home, secure an empty carriage then once in open country the dummy could be thrown away to the four winds – the last gesture. Pacified by this latest plan he shouldered the dummy as though it were a child, and walked slowly towards the booking office. No trains now mister, snow-blocked all the way up the line. Oh it's far worse up north, won't be clear for three or four days. Travelling in a circus or something Sir – looks a bit the worse for wear if I may say so. Eyes that set and reset in their symmetrical surroundings. Perhaps he ought to throw the thing away now, obviously causing curiosity; a suitable place must be found. The sea – of course, how simple, there it is, its smell drifting on to the platform, the sound of it wallowing over the town.

A yellow creeping sort of light spread across the station as Berg passed the waiting room, and looked in, saw the huddled shapes on the benches, several stretched out on a table like slabs of meat. No one moved: polyhedron somehow, Pompeii-risen.

Outside the gates he paused, gazing at the town set out before him, an unsorted puzzle that zig-zagged towards a motionless sea. He felt almost Lilliputian in comparison to the overcast sky, and the invading moon-craters that surrounded the station. Appearing across this unscarred landscape a familiar figure. Berg ducked behind the gates and flattened himself against the wall, holding the dummy across his arms, as though it were a ready sacrifice for some angry god. He heard the old man's metallic footsteps now on the bare patches of the road. Silence. Had he come upon a long stretch of snow-covered ground then, or had he stopped? Dare I look round? Best to wait for a moment or two. He lifted his head, as though to hear better, but the atmosphere became even more oppressive. Putting the dummy down, he peered round the gates: no one, absolutely deserted for streets and streets ahead. Where on earth had his father disappeared to, perhaps through another entrance to the station? In that case I must go, flee the place altogether. Why this eternal escaping? There isn't a thing they can justifiably accuse me of. Faces continually reappear; memory: the only sentiment allowed without emotional license. Letters, Proust-like to a friend, George into 'Georgina', the exchange of sonnets, in remembrance of Michelangelo, Rimbaud, Valéry, Whitman, occasionally Milton; you, Lycidas sleeping in the river valley, head cradled only by grass and the wind; body lulled by sunlight. Consolation, reassurance later with tea in the town, platefuls of cream cakes, doughnuts with sly clots of jam, and meringues with nipples on top. The furtive holding of hands with the one who lived in a distant house, with distant fearful parents, who went to church every Sunday, and presided over local committees. I'm a changeling really, my mother's an Eastern Queen, and my father's an Arab Prince, with a palace of gold in the desert and a hundred and one snow-white horses, that one day will belong to me. Watching the awe spring in the other's eyes, eyes that would never want to know a world existed outside the poplars that squared off the three-storeyed house on the hill.

> Of course their bread isn't any different from what you have here Aly; Mr. Dobbs supplies the whole neighbourhood, so don't keep saying theirs is any better than ours, because it's not true.

How could she be expected to know it was different, with a girl, for the first time, like a chicken plucked; coping with the endless chatter of periods, ponies, crushes, and the end of term dance? At first pillow-stained, later the sheets with a knowledge, the relief of self-stimulation.

Reaching the top of the hill he rested for a while and looked back. Like cuttle-fish ejecting their inky fluid, a group of men spread outside the station, and now approached the hill. The leading figure was unmistakeably the one with a scarred face; the last, slightly stooping figure, was no other than the old man. Berg quickly picked up the dummy and ran down the other side of the hill, gasping, shivering, the sweat standing out on his forehead and neck. He slowed down

Ann Quin

when entering the centre of the town, as though the very buildings shielded him in some way. They're out, of course, to get your blood, and God only knows what they might accuse you of now. Through silent white-edged streets, passing squat snowmen lined along the verges, or solidly standing in the middle of small backgardens. Now and then between houses he caught glimpses of the sea, so calm that it too appeared frozen. Sometimes there seemed to be no apparent familiar emblem of the town, the pier an ice palace looming out. He met no one as he made his way back. At last climbing the stairs, the dummy bouncing against him, he felt calmer, but hearing a movement on the landing, he paused, clutching the banisters for support. Is that you Nathy, Nathy darling is that you? Judith's flushed face appeared: a full moon flung suddenly from over a hill.

They hammered on the door, the partition shook. Pigeons stalked the window ledge. The idiots they'll never give up, but they'll never get in here, never. Whispering now, and for a while the knocking stopped, soon the whispering died down. He waited for them to begin again, but silence, everything quite still, remote. Goosepimples up the spine, along his arms. A pigeon pecked at the window, once, twice, until it became bored and flew off. Then as though through a loudspeaker his father's voice. Greb we know you're in there, open up, we're waiting Greb, do you hear, open the door. Silence. Berg rolled off the bed, put a chair and some books against the door.

What is it you want out of life Aly? Really I must say I don't understand you. I've slaved away, given you a good education, plus a decent home, and here you are selling hair tonic, you'll never make money out of it, and what good does it do?

Greb are you listening, open up, or we'll break this door down, do you hear? At least a hundred-foot drop from the window, the moon squashed between trees. If he opened the door they might—well might lynch, punch you into pulp, quite capable of brutality, that sadistic curl of the old man's mouth, of course that's what she, Judith, perhaps even Edith enjoyed, the brute force in him, yes that's what the majority of women presumably responded to, always a sacrifice, it had to be with them. How many were with the old man outside – and what a commotion?

He peered through the keyhole, saw his father standing between two men, all three beating their fists against the door. So he knows, they must have informed him, that evil-smelling scar-faced bum has spilt the beans. Well what of it, no one is without a fetish or two, if he succumbed, now and then, to an instinct that society declaimed, what's that in comparison to the thousand and one little perversions never splashed across the front page, that their next door neighbour performed, day in, day out, behind council walls, their snug clipped hedges, the aerial tightened after a storm? Greb if you don't open up at once we're going to break this door down do you hear? How dare he, the libidinous tone of the old man, how dare they intrude like this. What a diabolical liberty! Come now aren't you really enjoying the situation? Here you are trapped more or less, that for them at least you exist, that you have done something which is having an absolute positive result, an instant response, from not only one person but three, possibly four. Though it was, he had to admit, comparatively quiet next door, not a sound, the partition motionless. But his door continued jerking, and they were panting, grunting the other side. He jumped on to the bed, pressed against the partition. Back, then heavily forward, until the wood began giving way, a few more thrusts, and it would be down. He swayed on the bed for a moment, heard the shouts, fists and feet against the door. He swept up the dummy and with his elbows pushed once more against the wood, which broke apart. He jumped through, landing on their bed. Behind him still the noise of his door being kicked, any minute now and they would be upon him. He looked round, noticed the wardrobe door open, Judith's clothes, as usual, scattered about. He ran across the room, slipped, collided with some of the glass domes, which broke, their wax and stuffed objects rolled across the floor, some crushed as Berg scrambled over to the wardrobe.

> You're a good boy Aly in the way you always remember Mothers' Day. Those lovely daffodils you used to bring home. Good job Mr. Roberts never found out you had pinched them from his garden, still they had so many up there what's half a dozen to people like them?

Berg stepped inside the wardrobe, pushing the dummy into a corner, and squatting he edged the door until it was partially closed. Quick he's gone through, must be out in the street by now, get him for Crissake, get him before he destroys it completely. Berg winked at the dummy, then turned his attention to the six pairs of cracked boots that marched by, mud-spattered, sea-stained ragged trousers. He even saw a bald patch on his father's head. Then they had gone. The silence, after so much noise almost seemed unbearable. He remained where he was for some time until soon the retreating steps, a clock ticking made their impact, pressing him to leave his shelter, and emerge upon the debris of glass, crushed flowers, and the gap in the wall, where the partition had been, leaving sculptured wings clinging to the edges.

Where can I go now, it's obvious they'll be soon rampaging back? Even as he approached the door the stairs creaked, and soon he heard the familiar clicking along the landing, hesitate, presumably at his battered door, then click, click . . .

Judith stood in the doorway, staring at the broken glass, the broken pieces of wood scattered over the bed, the floor. Oh my God what a bloody awful mess, what a bloody one hell of a mess. Look couldn't she leave it all, go right away with him, forget everything, they could leave by the next train, find another place by the sea, they'd have one whale of a time, make a new life together, how about that? What a bloody awful mess, what a bloody fucking awful mess. Why couldn't they leave now, she wouldn't regret it, he promised that, give her anything, everything she wanted, why not try it at least for a while, not get married right away, but wait and see, how would that be, clear out of it all, what was the use of staying on here? What a bloody mess, look Aly clear out, on your own, do you hear, before I scream, scream, do you hear, now clear off. What a mess, oh Christ, Oh Jesus what an awful bloody mess. She advanced, and as though half blind from rage and tears, she stepped on some more of the glass objects, which cracked and jarred against each other, and their sealed treasures, at last free, sprang out, some like sea-anemones, or antennae, spreading into the rest of the disorder in the middle of the room. Berg stepped over them, avoiding the ones that still remained unbroken, and catching hold of Judith, he tried kissing her, but she pushed him away. They both looked down at the broken bits of glass, the flowers, insects, mice like matches, an owl with glass eye missing, lay on its side.

I don't know why you always want to break your cousin's nice toys, and that dolly Aly, that was Lotte's best one, given by her Uncle, now it was naughty you know of you to throw it down like that, and she'll never forgive you, never.

Of course even with the door locked, they could easily enter his room again, then through the gap. Perhaps it wasn't wise to stay much longer, and Judith presumably wasn't going to give way. Already the sound of steps on the landing, now outside. Silence. Silence. He stepped between the broken glass, the chairs, and stood by the bed, staring into his own room, at his slippers, the few bottles of hair tonic, the wigs on the dressing table, the curtain – a nun's veil fluttering into space. The convent kindergarten school, the sisters' smooth, marble faces, the warmth and safety at the sound of their rosaries as they swept into the chapel. The dark recesses, the sun spilling into pools on the altar. The deep satisfying security of it all. The solid hymn books, the shiny surface of new pews; the smell of incense, damp ancient walls. The icons where least expected, and the flowers drooping in candlelight. The resounding Angelus bell, the upward thrust of a pale ringless finger to equally pale lips. The bowed heads; the stifled giggles. But I don't believe in God, and how boring heaven must be just looking at His face, wouldn't hell be more fun?

    Oh my child, my child there's nothing more beautiful nothing more wonderful than looking upon God's face you will see. You will come to understand.

Aly who is it outside the door, Aly I'm frightened, sounds like a crowd outside, what do they want? Look she must shout out that everything was all right, that he Greb had gone to the station, they would find him there. She stared open-mouthed until he shook her. For her own sake she must do this. Her face and neck flushed, beads of sweat ran into the corners of her mouth. She shouted out exactly what he had told her. Soon his father's gruff answer, Judith's eyes widened.

It's him Nathy, Nath . . . Berg silencing her with his hand, pushed her on to the bed, holding her there until he was sure his pursuers had left. Sighing he released Judith, but pressed her trembling fingers to his mouth. Instantly aware of a wave of nausea, which could not at first be accounted for. He circled some freckles on her wrist, and three vertically running from the knuckle-bone. If she now speaks, the nausea will rise. But her head averted, Judith sat upright, mouth firmly closed, her fingers stiff. How does she really feel, what is she thinking? A moment ago yes I am willing to admit it, the nausea had been caused by an acute attack of boredom, the futility of everything, especially the game of human relationships: the fact that she had obeyed him, reacted exactly as imagined, and brought him back into the circle of himself. But now, right now, he couldn't be sure of what to expect. If he should stand up, walk out, leave this instant, would she demand some explanation of what had happened, what he wanted of her, where he might be going, or would she remain silent, neither accepting or rejecting, giving no release to his ambivalence? Isn't she the very prototype of the woman one dreams of being caught up by, at rest in her omnipotence, knowing her to be ruthless, but never accepting the fact, half the fascination in wondering how far she will go – the wiles, lies, all the vanities accepted, but never quite confronted? The so-called mystery of a woman, so involved in the many-sided portraits of herself, eternally eluding one's grasp, knowing she would lose all if she ever showed her true identity, her real worth. Love is purely a temporary artifice, and why should I disregard the fact, why should I desire to be in the throes of illusion, when I know that love comes in disguises and is rarely recognised at the time or ever appreciated? Oh Aly you've bruised me, look three marks already, and one on my arm. Wait a minute, it's so uncomfortable like this. He watched her bend, and wriggle her underwear off. There that's better. Oh Aly make it last, he never could you know, well not more than – oh you are gorgeous, so big, so beautiful there, oh it does feel good to be with you Aly, do you love me, say you love me a little Aly won't you?

Like entering the sea. The sea alone. Alone by the sea. By the sea. Alone. By yourself. Oh it's nice when you do that, do it again, oh it's lovely. Nathy, oh Nathy my darling.

The gap in the wall seemed wider from the angle of his head. He closed his eyes.

Look Aly there's some more glass, do be careful going about like that on your bare feet. Oh look at my poor flowers, the mice as well, and I do believe the owl's feathers are moulting. Bending, kneeling, crawling between the chairs and the velvet-covered couch, where I can sit and smoke a pipe in an evening, while she combs her hair. The gap now covered up by an old sheet, which flapped if the window was open. The door bolted. They hadn't returned. Not yet. Berg pressed his face against the window, the snow had practically melted now. Tonight would be the best time, when Judith slept, leave the town, away from this annihilation of domesticity. Strange how the sheet covering that space flapped, wasn't the window closed? No accounting for draughts in a house like this, rotting with woodworm no doubt and dry rot, most places by the sea were; damp, cold. A place where the sun shines day in, day out, that would be it, Paradise. How much money did Judith really have, perhaps after all he should stay, then clear off, go abroad, Italy, yes that seemed the place. Those brochures that one looked at secretly, while having to thumb through coach tours to the North, to the West.

We must try and go away this year Aly, somewhere quiet, just the two of us, by the sea, or wherever you fancy, it would be nice wouldn't it?

He watched Judith smooth the owl's feathers down. I must say Aly you're a strange fellow, really sometimes I can't make you out, it's as though you are always playing a part. Funny thing is Nathy's a bit like that you know. He told me once that he went to a psychiatrist, taking a friend's place, for a lark, he said, and in just the one session she told him he always had to dramatise every situation because he had missed his true vocation, he should have gone on the stage. I let him make that ghastly dummy because I thought oh well it will keep him amused, but when the thing almost seemed to obsess him, even more than that bloody budgie well then I began to wonder, yes I really did. Oh I forgot to tell you Aly it was that they found in the rug, a bloody dummy, not a body at all, imagine you thought and so did I that . . . Not a body at all ah well what did I expect, after all there had been the discovery of the thing at the station, they had all known of course. Berg stared at his hands; hands drawing a circle on the window, hands springing over a woman's shoulders, shaking a rag doll, now plucking feathers round the room. Oh Aly stop that, are you crazy, have you gone completely up the wall? Yes it's true, Lor' only knows where it is now, but you remember the time you went off to the station, well I followed you, saw you put the – well you know what in the luggage place, of all places, and then as luck would have it, you dropped the ticket, and some chap with a scar down his face, yes I remember him, how ugly he was ugh – anyway he waited until you had disappeared, then he went and collected the thing, they unrolled it there and then – you can imagine how I felt when I saw what the bloody thing was, Oh Aly you should have seen their faces, even the station master laughed. I didn't wait to see what they did with it, pity really if it's lost, because it had one of Nathy's best suits on. I can remember him putting it on the beastly thing, and what a scene there was because of a button missing, I had to sew one on, on a bloody dummy would you believe it? Anyway I was thankful it wasn't a dead body you had been carting around. Here Aly where are you going, what on earth are you doing in the wardrobe love? Oh Lor' there it is like Christ risen again, get it out of the way Aly, it really gives me the shivers, it seems to haunt us wherever we go. Look give it to me I'll take it down to the basement and put it in the dustbin, but take that suit off, after all it's a good one even though it's singed, torn in places, that can soon be mended, and we'll get it cleaned, might come in handy for you, I can lengthen the trousers, you don't need turnups these days. I do like seeing men in slightly tight trousers, can be quite effective, sort of sexy don't you think? Well don't just stand there holding it, look give it to me, oh Aly don't take it down without taking that suit off, what a waste, Aly did you hear me?

Her voice hurtled after him down the stairs; the door swinging in a rising wind. The snow completely gone. He would put the dummy behind a breakwater, then the tide would carry it away. He approached the biggest, and longest breakwater, but squatting the other side were two men. He scuttled back, dragging the dummy across the pebbles, under the pier, where the sand like dust slightly stirred, and his shadow strung over the crosswork of black iron-grids. The gush of a sewer nearby drove him out on to the open beach once more. The line of lamps from the Front disappeared, leaving you with a dream of a blind lobster zig-zagging across the sands, groping, you mounted a horse, which refused to move, looking down you noticed the animal had only two claws on which to travel, and below these the pebbles had changed into a thousand eyeless birds with hollow breasts, trying to sing. What was that? Perhaps only the echo of his own foot falls, occasionally the cry of gulls, the tip of a white wing. He dug his fingers into his pockets and started whistling. He'd dump the dummy round the jutting piece of cliff, once behind that, no one, could possibly see what went on. The moon sprang out, as though torn in half, shedding a pale light upon the rocks – prophets' heads – surrounding him. Aware of a shadow out of place, a shadow that fell across his own. He looked round: a deserted beach. But there again, a vast shadow thrown in a slanting way to his right now. He moved a step or two, then halted. Was he being followed, perhaps someone had seen him? In the act of pouncing maybe, right this minute, lurking behind a rock, and behind another one the old man probably signalling instructions. Down with him, tear him to shreds, he's not human, such things as he does, assaults my woman, takes his pleasure how and where he can find it, blasted pimp, screw him good and proper, throw him to the gulls, the sea can lap up his remains. He walked on, head averted from the spray, the increasing mist. Waves now pounded in, the sand snaked swiftly between the pebbles. He looked back once, half hoping someone would be following, almost a relief to have seen something, anyone.

He threw the dummy down, but did not hear it touch the ground, as if in fact it had been thrown down a well, still falling through endless space. He peered into the darkness. But why bother any more, surely an important factor was that he could now no longer be held responsible for it? As though I'm still thinking, acting in terms of a dead body, yes, going on as though it had been something real, made out of flesh and blood, something that will eventually turn into dust, when it's only something made of some sort of rubbery plastic stuff, that's all. He wiped his fingers on his coat, and went to shelter against the cliff, staring at the only thing he could see: his hands.

Beyond these, illuminated by past summers, one summer remained that stayed the sun long into the night after you had watched the others; others with their fathers knee-deep, belly-button unconcerned, roly-poly mothers stretching out of the sea. Whiter than starch hands on bat and ball, you failed to catch. Tents, buckets, spades; others that went on digging barricades. You castle-bound, spying on princesses, honey-gold, singing against the blue, if touched surely their skin would ooze? Aware of own smell, skin-texture, sun in eyes, lips, toes, the softness underneath, in between, wondering what miracle made you, the sky, the sea. Conscious of sound, gulls hovering, crying, or silent at rarer intervals, their swift turns before being swallowed by the waves. Then no sound, all suddenly would be soundless, treading softly, dividing rocks with fins, and sword-fish fingers plucking away clothes, that were left with your anatomy, huddled like ruffled birds waiting. A chrysalis heart formed on the water's surface, away from the hard-polished pebbles, sand-blowing and elongated shadows. Away, faster than air itself, dragon-whirled. Be given to, the sliding of water, to forget, be forgotten; premature thoughts – predetermined action. In a moment fixed between one wave and the next, the outline of what might be ahead. On your back, staring into space, becoming part of the sky, a speckled bird's breast that opened up at the slightest notion on your part. But the hands, remember the hands that pulled your legs, that doubled you up, and dragged you down? Surprised at non-resistance. Voices that called, creating confusion. Cells tighter than shells, you spinning into spirals, quick-silver, thrashing the water, making stars scatter. Narcissus above, staring at a shadow-bat spreading out, finally disappearing into the very centre of the ocean. They were always there waiting by the edge, behind them the cliffs extended. Your head disembodied, bouncing above

the separate force of arms and legs, rhythmical, the glorious
sensation of weightlessness, moon-controlled, and far below
your heart went on exploring, no matter how many years came
between, nor how many people were thrust into focus. That
had surely been the beginning, the separating of yourself from
the world that no longer revolved round you, the awareness
of becoming part of, merging into something else, no longer
dependent upon anyone, a freedom that found its own reality,
half of you the constant guardian, watching your actions, your
responses, what you accepted, what you might reject.

Three shadows engulfed his. He swayed across the beach to
the water's edge. There he is, get him, ah this time we've got
you Greb, you won't get away now. The water came as a shock.
He went under as he heard their cries, the cry of gulls. He
came up. The cliffs petrified. He heard a splash, then another,
nearby; had they decided to follow him – actually dived in
after him? No, only a pebble, followed by a few more that
showered over him, one hitting the side of his head. He spun
round, and noticed a storm lantern swinging – chalice lit by a
stained-glass sun – gliding over the waves. Damn they have a
boat already, so soon, so soon. He dived further, deeper, gain-
ing invisible depths; falling into more than silence, or space,
or sleep, non-human, not breathing, lungs part of response,
reflex-controlled, and if I stayed under? They would presumably wait for him to rise, emerge. He drifted up to the surface,
then took pleasure in diving back suddenly while their light
bobbed nearer, their oars sliced up the waves; taking delight
in feeding off their sadism, the lure of the victim leading
them to their own destruction. If I could only be Prospero, for
a minute, create a storm, that would devour the boat, fling
them, the old man over and beyond seven seas – those are
stones that were his eyes.

His face lapping up the waves, bird dislocated, mute, motionless, wondering at the unpredictable situations he found himself in, or the predictable actions of those now silent in the boat tossed in another direction. The reflection of their light fell away from a dark shape that heaved itself on to a rock. He could no longer see the boat, the moon behind a huge mass of clouds. He stood on the rock, shivering, trying to gain enough breath and energy to make the journey in shore.

Carried by a single wave; the rain fell locust-like as he scrambled up the beach and into the shelter of the cliffs. Cursing his wet clothes, and the fact that he couldn't even have a decent cigarette, and far too tired to attempt the walk back, he leaned against the cliff, watching the lightning travel swiftly across the sea, along the shore, and for a moment flash upon the pier and Front. So it's still there, that world, a town I came to and . . .

Alistair Greb you are accused of attempt to murder. Bring in the evidence. It's in some seaside resort your Ludship, the accused said he had gone there in order to find his father. Bring in the next witness. Edith Mildred Berg is this your son?

Oh Aly how could you, God's still in his heaven you know, some of us forget that.

Next witness please. Judith Helen Goldstein do you know the accused?

Aly you should have saved the suit at least.

His head sank as the cliff fell away.

A face, an eye, a hand half hanging off. Berg stared at the dummy that lay two feet away, covered in sand and seaweed. Farther down the upturned boat – a huge beetle on its back. Tiny ripples of water caught the sun turning it over gently, silver-glinting fish in pools and the sudden movement of a crab stirred the sand. Berg walked slowly down to the boat, and tried turning it keel up. Drift over the ocean, the Atlantic, the Adriatic, oblivion where are you? But the boat did not move an inch, some water from inside splashed over as Berg continued pushing. Several gulls circled above cat-howling. Spreading his arms out he flapped and squawked until they circled away. Though two of the biggest birds swooped, and began pecking savagely at something, which already other gulls had ferociously attacked. He walked over, still flapping his arms, the birds angrily beat their wings, their beaks snapping the air as they left their prey. Berg stared at the eyeless corpse for some time before recognising it to be one of his pursuers. He looked up and down the beach. Had the others been washed up too?

Or only this one for the birds the other two for the fish? He quickly searched the pockets, a few papers which he tore up, as he did so he noticed the scar running from the left ear to the jaw, he kicked the body over face down, and proceeded up the beach. Some gulls hovered this time above the dummy, one of the gulls, in fact, seemed intent upon pecking at the suit. Berg waved them off, but the biggest still remained, he flapped and squawked at it, until it left, but only to wait a little way off, and once he thought it would swoop down on to his head, wings whirring like an electric fan. He caught hold of the dummy's legs and dragged it towards the sea, the head suddenly bounced off and rolled into the water. The gull furiously swooped on to it as the waves carried them both out to sea. Berg propped what remained of the dummy against the boat, and brushing himself down he walked along by the edge of the water.

I have to report my father's missing. How long has he been missing sir? Twenty-eight years. That's a long time for someone to be missing and you only reporting his loss now sir? He passed the gulls so intent upon their victim they were hardly aware of his approach. I won't look; there were dark little cages where the skin had been rubbed or eaten away near the neck, the clothes already in strips, where the birds had pecked. Berg waved his arms half-heartedly, one or two of the gulls fluttered off, or wobbled away, standing now at a short distance eyeing him. A few birds perched on the boat. He walked back, picked the dummy up and threw it into the sea, watching it bob on the waves, head-less, a tree's stump, ignored by the birds. Approaching the pier on the steps he saw Judith waving. Aly, Aly where on earth have you been? I've looked for you everywhere, I was so terribly worried, what did you do with that thing eh? I noticed you hadn't put it in the dustbin as I said, so I guessed you would have brought it down here. I waited until daylight, and when you hadn't come back well I came straight down. My God Aly you do look a sight, really you do, what's come over you, what's possessed you? Better come straight back now, you're all wet, what in heaven's name have you been up to?

Oh look at your lovely new coat all that muck on your trousers too. Oh Aly I told you not to go climbing with Billy in your nice new things, now I'm not going to buy you anything else, what will the Deals say?

Oh I nearly forgot this, a letter for you Aly, looks as though it's been lying around for days. Yes we'll get back, have a nice pot of tea. Your hair's like seaweed, and your poor hands Aly they're absolutely freezing.

My darling Aly,

I've not heard from you for a long time now, at least two weeks Aly boy, and I worry about you when I don't get a letter, you ought to write dear, you know you mean all the world to me. I hope you are all right?

You must remember Aly to keep warm in this cold weather. Are you wearing the woolly underwear I sent?

You will be pleased to hear that Lotte's expecting, of course Alf is very pleased about it all, he says he wants a girl, but Lotte, I think, wants a boy. Doreen, you remember Doreen don't you, well she's getting married to Billy your old school mate, you know the one that gave you those flower things and said they were peas, and you had those nasty worms for ever so long afterwards. Oh dear I nearly forgot, you'll never guess who's just written, yes him, Aly, your father, just like him out of the blue, and guess what, he wants to come and visit us.

Well, of course, it gave me quite a turn. I wondered if you had seen and spoken to him, persuaded him to come back or something? He doesn't mention having met you or anything. I must say seeing his writing gave me a funny feeling, and Aly, I think he needs me, he seems to be in some sort of trouble, I can always sense it, even though he doesn't actually mention anything in his letter. At night I think I hear him calling out to me. I haven't the heart to turn him down, perhaps he could come just for a little while? I mean I could never really settle down living with him again, though mind you it would be nice to see him, maybe he could come for Christmas? Anyway I won't reply until I've heard from you, as I thought I would like to know what you think, and maybe you could even talk the matter over with him, as you're so near. He's staying at the Seaview hotel. Why don't you call on him Aly, as you're so close, he'd be ever so pleased, I'm sure, to see you. Anyway I'll leave that for you to decide. I wish you could have been home last weekend, it was simply glorious. I took our favourite walk on Sunday into Southfield, and had some nice tea and crumpets there. Well that's all for the moment. Look after yourself Aly, and please write to your old Mum soon won't you? Let me know when you'll be home, and I'll meet you at the station, and also let me know about you know who?

All my love darling boy,

your loving Mumsie

Berg read the letter twice, before carefully folding it up and tucking it into his breast pocket. He sat sipping a mug of tea, while Judith frowned over a frying pan. Awful draught through that gap Aly, perhaps you could put a piece of wood there.

Not much of a one your father round the house, and do you know he used to paint right round all the pictures, made me feel quite ashamed when we had to leave, I mean to say what would the new tenants think, those great big bare patches all over the living room walls, and the bedrooms too?

All right, all right I didn't mean right this minute Aly, but it better be done soon before old Mrs. Whatsaname finds out. Funny about Nathy not appearing, perhaps he really has gone for good now, ah well one door closes another one opens I always say. Perhaps we can look for another place Aly, a nice little self-contained flat, I'm sick to death of cooking, eating, living in just this room. You can get a good job, there's any number going during the holiday season. Pass that fork love, and set the table, it's nearly ready.

They sat opposite each other. He heard her munching, breaking up the toast. I always forget, two or three lumps Aly? Under her dress were the bruises still there? Oh love not now, stop it Aly not over breakfast. He watched his hands apply themselves, his mouth covering the purple patches between the nipples, his teeth sinking in, as she moaned and swayed in the chair. Oh you are a one really, fancy at this time of day, he never would, you know, never, not as early as . . . He pressed his fingers between, into a darkness, wet, soft, yielding. Someone laughed, tumbled into the softness. The sheet covering the gap, where the partition had been, began flapping, and for a moment, yes there, just now, a face between the jagged edges of wood. Aly what's the matter, what are you doing now for God's sake? He swept back the sheet covering, stared into his room, at the door swinging on hinges. He climbed over the bed and entered, then out to the landing. Was that the front door closing? Aly what do you think you're up to, looking for a ghost or something? Come on, come and finish your toast and marmalade won't you?

Yes let's have a proper meal, with a proper woman sitting opposite, with a proper plastic table cloth, a proper pink, with proper yellow cups and saucers, and a proper clock ticking over with the proper time. Because he's not coming back, he'll never be back, because he's full fathoms five. For why should he intrude now when he was never there when the blades of corn struck the wind, and the trees whispered go home, go home, the hour of play is over, away from the tree's trunk with its skin of a toad, the bees swarming below; bees with ruby eyes that would fly in after the goodnight kiss and the door closed. A glimpse of the village clock facing the sea. A silent invasion of fish after midnight on the hill, staring into the valley. Yes he had been in another darkness, lifting the banks from rivers, letting the earth slide through his hands, while you in the house danced through the bead curtains, which slowly unthreaded, while the weeds sprang towards the windows, and the gate sang when the fence, like ribs, fell on the rockery where the wallflowers gently insisted, and the dandelions retained something of a smile. He unwound the sheet where he had thrown it on the bed, and nailed it either side so that it covered the gap in the wall once more. He weaved silently round the room – a salamander, whose incandescent spirit possessed the gift of a thousand lives.

At last the newspaper item appeared, bottom left on the second page. A man's body, presumably aged between fifty-five and sixty, has been found washed up on the beach on the west side of the pier. So far he has not been identified.

Aly don't forget you promised to run down and buy some bread. While passing you might drop in and pay the rent, else she'll be up asking for it, and I don't want her to see this mess before you do something about clearing it up, and mending the partition.

Berg tucked the newspaper under his arm, and whistling, he went out. What did you say his name was, Berg? That's funny, we had a summons for someone of that name, hadn't paid his hotel bill, stole a few things as well I believe sir, well I'm sorry if he's your father, we'll soon see, except of course he's a bit unidentifiable, the sea's mucked him about. Is there anything you can go by, any marks, scars or anything like that? A scar you say, running from his left ear to the jaw, a deep one?

Well we'll just go down and see sir.

The eyeless face once again a sock's heel with holes. Yes there's certainly a scar where you said sir, I am sorry, mother still alive eh? Gently does it now, need a stiff one after that, but perhaps you could come along and give me a few more particulars, seeing, well seeing he's a relative and so on.

He emerged upon a town that was dazed by half a day's sun. He walked on to the pier, walked to the end where the ghost train was, where a man with puffed red cheeks sat doing football pools in his glass box, and handed Berg a ticket without looking up. He sat in a carriage, felt the train start up, there was no one else on it. He closed his eyes, felt the carriage jerk, stop, shudder, a cackle, and some moaning, and the carriage almost seemed to separate, spin on its own. He kept his eyes closed, as it continued to jolt, and the sound of laughter, of wind through opening, closing doors. Here Mister you've come through, or do you want another go? Right you are then, that'll be another bob's worth. He penetrated the darkness, stared at the skulls thrust out at him, the spiders that hung down, the coloured lights, the green and red eyes, and laughter that sounded like Judith's. Had enough this time Mister, had enough?

He bought some fish and chips, and sat at the end of the pier, dipping his fingers into the mound of newspaper, wiping his fingers on filmstars, models' legs, and half attempted the crossword puzzle. The sea changed from blue to purple, through the grating of the pier he watched the water lap the black patchwork below. He decided to buy a postcard and took a long time in choosing one, a coloured picture of the whole seafront.

Hallo Mum,

Just a line to say I shall be staying on for a while longer here. It's quite nice and sunny today, wish you were here. Received your letter, which I shall answer soon.

All love,

Your own Aly

He bought a glittering butterfly brooch, wrapped in tissue paper, in a silver-papered box.

Oh Aly you haven't brought the bread, and I bet you didn't pay the rent, she came up, and I had to give her some money to keep her quiet, all ready for a dreadful scene, especially when she saw your door broken, the partition as well. I told a bit of a tale, said some thugs had followed you, beaten you up, taken your things, that you were staying with me. She seemed pacified by the story anyway, at least after I gave her the money, didn't even enquire after Nathy, though the old bitch will probably be sniffing round our heels I bet. Oh Aly let's get out soon. You are naughty though not getting the bread. Oh love how sweet of you, oh Aly what is it? Ah there, isn't that lovely, it will go with my purple, look won't it sweetie? Just a moment and I'll try it on, then you can see. But do pop down love and give her the rent, or she'll be up again. You've still got it haven't you Aly? Oh no, not two weeks' rent, you couldn't have spent all that, not in a couple of hours surely, what have you been doing, other than buying presents? This brooch couldn't have cost that much, the pin's crooked. Here you better take this, tell her she'll get the rest on Saturday, my alimony hasn't come in for this week yet. What? Yes of course he's still alive I told you, separated in '55, but the least said about him. Now go on with you Aly, and for goodness sake come straight back.

Black his footprints on the stairs, his shadow breaking up the walls. Outside vestiges of dry leaves, between the twigs that spread into triangles, a twisting mass of brown dribbling under the trees. Mr. Greb, hey Mr. Greb, Mrs. Goldstein says you have some rent money for me. Oh I was sorry to hear about you being beaten up like that Mr. Greb, terrible things happen these days, you can never tell when it's your last step can you? Of course there'll be quite a bit to pay, for a new door, then there's the partition. You see it's all got to be done up very soon I've a gentleman moving in there, he's even left his luggage in the hall, so you see I've got to tidy things up a bit before he moves in. I understand you're staying with Mrs. Goldstein for a few days, that is until you find another place, well of course that will be extra, it's not really meant for two, it's hardly a double room, but I make concessions, yes just now and then. Mind those things Mr. Greb near the stairs, well that's a silly place to put his stuff isn't it, that's right put the cage over there, it'll be quite safe there.

Of course bird cages look all the same, if you pass them in a shop, they all have gilt edges round the doors and little silver bells – but mirrors cracked, and dry yellow feathers clinging round the edges? Said he was going to get a budgie stuffed, funny how most of my tenants like to keep pets, not all stuffed mind you. Just over three quid he said it cost – cheap I suppose when you don't have to feed a stuffed one. By the way you wouldn't know anything about Mr. Berg, I didn't like to ask her, as I thought – oh I see, goodness I am sorry, nice old chap really, had his ways you know, like most of us I suppose. Funny thing is my new tenant now, the one who's moving into the room you used to have, reminds me a little of Mr. Berg, first thing I thought when he entered the house, carrying that cage, why there's the old man himself, I must ask him for the rent. But then this one's got a beard, looks older too, and I don't mind telling you either, he's more classy, and I hope has a bit more money, well we have to be careful who we take in don't we? What with all these delinquents about the town, you never know if it's your last sleep, still I must say this new lodger looks a harmless sort of chap, says he's starting up a chiropody place in the town with some friend, hopes to make it quite a business – well I suppose people do complain about their feet a lot. How's the hair business these days Mr. Greb?

Head nodding, feet scraping the stairs, her voice in the distance. Aly what's kept you, what's that old hag been saying, gossiping I bet about everyone? Look I've fixed up a temporary piece of wood, until we get a proper partition up, if I know her she'll be having someone taking over that room of yours before the day's out. Well you haven't said anything, you haven't even noticed Aly, look doesn't the brooch look nice? Oh no, no it's quite all right where it is, oh don't pin it there, it looks almost obscene, you are a one, really you are. What do you want for lunch Aly, meat or fish? Of course the fishmongers will be closed, though you could run down and get a couple of chops. Aly, oh no Aly stop it now, you are naughty, really you are, not now, it's nearly lunch time, aren't you hungry? Aly there's some potatoes over there that need peeling. Aly don't you think we ought to have new curtains, and sweetie you won't mind will you, but I've ordered a cat, a nice brand new Siamese one, I went into the pet shop this morning and spoke to the man, he said he had one coming in the day after tomorrow. Aly what do you think we should call it? Aly oh no, don't not now, hush, listen, did you hear something? Aly there's someone next door, I can hear them moving about. There what did I tell you, I knew she'd have someone moved in there next to no time. Aly love what are you staring at?

A window just cleaned. Above the sea, overlooking a town, a man motionless, bound by a velvet-covered couch, and a woman, whose hands flutter round a butterfly brooch. They stare at a piece of wood, five foot by seven, that shakes now and then – an animal thumping its tail . . .

Dear readers,

As well as relying on bookshop sales, And Other Stories relies on subscriptions from people like you for many of our books, whose stories other publishers often consider too risky to take on.

Our subscribers don't just make the books physically happen. They also help us approach booksellers, because we can demonstrate that our books already have readers and fans. And they give us the security to publish in line with our values, which are collaborative, imaginative and 'shamelessly literary'.

All of our subscribers:

- receive a first-edition copy of each of the books they subscribe to
- are thanked by name at the end of our subscriber-supported books
- receive little extras from us by way of thank you, for example: postcards created by our authors

BECOME A SUBSCRIBER,
OR GIVE A SUBSCRIPTION TO A FRIEND

Visit andotherstories.org/subscriptions to help make our books happen. You can subscribe to books we're in the process of making. To purchase books we have already published, we urge you to support your local or favourite bookshop and order directly from them – the often unsung heroes of publishing.

OTHER WAYS TO GET INVOLVED

If you'd like to know about upcoming events and reading groups (our foreign-language reading groups help us choose books to publish, for example) you can:

- join our mailing list at: andotherstories.org
- follow us on Twitter: @andothertweets
- join us on Facebook: facebook.com/AndOtherStoriesBooks
- admire our books on Instagram: @andotherpics
- follow our blog: andotherstories.org/ampersand

Current & Upcoming Books

ANN QUIN (1936–1973) was a British writer from Brighton. She was prominent amongst a group of British experimental writers of the 1960s, which included BS Johnson. Prior to her death in 1973, she published four novels: *Berg* (1964), *Three* (1966), *Passages* (1969) and *Tripticks* (1972). A collection of short stories and fragments, *The Unmapped Country* (edited by Jennifer Hodgson), was published by And Other Stories in 2018.